Kidnap

by **Neil Colby**

Kidnap

Editor: D.S. Williams (The Pedantic Punctuator)
Cover designer: W. Goulart

ISBN: 9780994406644

Neil Colby,
PO Box K712
Haymarket
New South Wales 1240
Australia

neilcolby.com

In memory of Marlene

1

Along cloud hung motionless in an otherwise clear sky, signalling a near-perfect spring day. Jasper Owen sat near the hangar, sipping his coffee. He had a view of the Blue Goose anchored on to the jetty and, beyond it, Cornet Harbour and an expanse of silvery blue water stretching all the way to the horizon. The strong coffee was having the same effect as if someone had stuck a pair of defibrillator pads to his chest and pressed the triggers. Owen took a deep breath of air, enjoying its saltiness. Some mornings were certainly worth getting up for.

A large Mercedes Benz, black, turned into the gates and aimed straight for the hangar, its wheels kicking up little clouds of dust as it accelerated and then slowed to stop about twenty metres from where Jasper was sitting. He eyed it curiously. *This client had money,* he decided.

He rose lazily to his feet, as a man in an Armani suit opened the rear passenger door and let himself out. *What? No chauffeur to open the door for him?* Owen was almost disappointed.

Jasper nodded with a "Morning" when the man walked closer. He eyed the man's shoes, which were polished to such a high gloss that they mirrored the sky.

"Mister Owen? You're the pilot, right?"

Jasper nodded again. "Only one in Cornet Harbour."

The man grinned. "I heard there was another, about five miles from here. Fellow by the name of Andrews?"

Jasper nodded sourly. "Bruce. Yes," he said. "He's okay if you want a tour around the harbour."

The man put out his hand with a smile. "I'm looking at a longer trip than that," he said.

"You're not Australian," Jasper pointed out, picking the man's Midwestern American accent.

"'Fraid not," the man said, without explaining where he was from. Instead he gestured towards the Blue Goose. "Is that the plane?"

"That's her. A De Havilland Canada DHC-6-300 Twin Otter."

"Nice," the man responded.

"I spoke to your secretary on the phone. She didn't mention your name," said Jasper.

"Personal assistant," the man corrected. "Sandra handles all my affairs. Everything. The best there is," said the man.

Jasper smiled complacently. *You're screwing her, aren't you?* He was close to saying it aloud.

"Call me Edgewood," the man said. "Clive."

"Want a seat?" said Jasper. He gestured towards a wooden chair, positioned next to his own.

"Don't mind if I do."

Jasper waited for Clive Edgewood to sit down. The man was not in a hurry, and seemed quite confident and at ease with himself. He selected a cheroot from a slender cigar holder in his jacket pocket and lit it, watching Jasper as he did so.

"Care for one?"

Jasper shook his head.

"Can't resist them. I grew up on a diet of spaghetti westerns," Clive said with a smirk.

Jasper knew the movies well. Clint Eastwood; 'The Man With No Name'. *Seemed appropriate for a man who was almost certainly lying about his own name*, he thought.

"So you've got quite a range, I take it?" said Clive, nodding at the Goose.

Jasper nodded. "About 700 nautical miles," he said. "After that, you'll need specially fitted fuel tanks. Otherwise, we can stop and refuel on one of the islands. Where are you thinking of going?"

Clive smiled. "Let's say I have a client who prefers to keep the flight path confidential for the time being…" he said. "The range sounds about right, though."

"We've got to log the flight. You know that, right?"

"Of course. Only, we may have to divert from the path just a tad."

Jasper took a large gulp of coffee, and allowed it to settle in his stomach before replying. "Let me save us both a lot of time. Coastal patrols are active in this area. There's a people-smuggling problem here, and the navy is keeping watch. It's plain stupid to get involved in anything illegal. So, whatever you're about to tell me—"

"Hang on there, big fella. You're getting way ahead of yourself. I'm not smuggling anything, alright? Truth is, I made a promise to someone I hold very dear, and I'm trying to fulfil that promise."

Jasper put the coffee mug down, and sat back in his chair. He was willing to listen, for the time being anyway.

Clive began to explain. "My uncle Frank was a great man. He came to my rescue when my parents kicked me out. He raised me from the age of six. The man was my hero; my one true role model. But then he got himself mixed up with a bad crowd, and they took everything off him. Framed him, and left him to rot in jail. I tried to get him out, on parole, in any way that I could. Hired the best lawyers; they couldn't do a damn thing. Then, after fifteen long years, they signed his release. Two days before he got out, he died in his cell. Heart attack."

"I'm sorry," Jasper muttered.

"That man had only one dream. He wanted to go back to the Manuca Islands. He had a woman there once, but she left him when he got himself thrown in jail. But he always wanted to go back. He begged me to take him, once he got out, no matter what the cost. But now he's dead. The only thing I can still do for him is to take his body out there, and bury him."

Jasper nodded. "I understand. It sounds like all you need to do is get the paperwork sorted, and I'll fly his body out there for you."

Clive shook his head. "No can do. He had a criminal record, so I'm not allowed to move his body across the border, not even to the islands."

"Maybe you can package his ashes …"

Clive shook his head vehemently. "I can't do that to Frank. He hated the idea of being cremated. He was dead against it."

Jasper thought about the man's dilemma for a moment, and then shook his head. "It's still illegal, mate. I just can't do it."

"Hey, I understand, believe me. Last thing you want to do

is get yourself tangled up in a thing like this..." said Clive, "... without suitable reward. Which is why I'm prepared to make you a handsome offer."

Jasper held up his hand in protest, but Clive was insistent. "Just hear me out," he said. "Then you can make up your mind. If you're not interested, I'll walk away and go ask someone else."

Jasper shrugged lightly, and Clive leaned forward, as if he was going to share some intimate secret.

"Tell me if I'm on the wrong track here," said Clive, watching Jasper's face closely. "I'm thinking you're a good pilot and you run a good, profitable business. Only thing is, you're running somebody else's business. Maybe someone who doesn't appreciate your talents as much as he should..."

Jasper listened, but he didn't respond.

"Now I'm thinking someone like you deserves an opportunity. What if an angel investor makes a substantial investment in the business – *your* business? What if that same investor puts in a good word with the manager of a leading bank, and gets you a low-interest business loan to cover the rest? All above board, legal, signed and sealed?"

Clive glanced over at the Blue Goose and then back at Jasper. "How much for one of those? Ten million?"

"Seven million, new," replied Jasper. He flashed an amused smile in Clive's direction.

"An investment of four million would be good start, let's say for a twenty five percent stake in the business. That way we'd be business partners, and I'd help you every step of the way because it would be good for me too."

"Sounds generous, but I don't fancy the jail time much," said Jasper.

"Then let me tell you about Guido Ramos," said Clive, his eyes twinkling. "He flew contraband to the Indonesian islands – made quite a good profit too, particularly on the abalone. They caught him, and threatened him with jail time. As it turned out, with a good lawyer, he was fined seventy thousand dollars. That's chickenfeed, my friend. And I happen to be acquainted with a whole shark tank of good lawyers. They won't break a sweat to get you to walk free – and that's in the extremely unlikely event of you being caught."

"In theory, maybe. They put people smugglers away for life. For all I know, body smugglers fall into the same category," said Jasper. His smile turned sour.

"Do you know of any actual cases?" said Clive, watching Jasper's expression carefully. "You don't, do you? That would be because there ain't none. You would not be smuggling anything – just doing a friend a favour, at extremely low risk."

Jasper shook his head again, this time flashing a grin.

Clive stood up, and held out a business card to him. "My private number. Call me any time. But I'm out of here tomorrow, so I'll need your answer by sundown."

Jasper took the card and stared at it. It was black, with embossed, ivory-coloured lettering. Expensive printing.

"I've been in business for a long time," said Clive, "and I never back the wrong horse. So far, it has worked out pretty sweet for me and my business partners."

Jasper watched him sceptically.

Clive seemed unaffected. "Did I mention the business comes with no strings attached? This is a one-time favour, and I'm prepared to pay handsomely for it. After that, you are the master of your own destiny. Me, I'll simply be a silent partner. You make the decisions. Say yes, and you'll have a signed contract in your hands within twelve hours."

Jasper stood up too. "I'll have to think—"

"It's one of those opportunities that will happen once in your life," Clive interrupted. "Grab it, or lose it ... forever."

Clive stepped backwards. "Good to meet you," he said with a nod of the head. Then he turned and headed back to his car, settling into the back seat. The Mercedes sped off and again left a small dust cloud trailing behind it.

2

When the chartered plane touched down at Sydney International Airport, Norman Brassington was quick to get out of his plush seat. He was a large man, and didn't relish being squashed into a flying tin can, no matter how luxurious, for hours on end. The flight from London was pure torture, and he was relieved to be back on terra firma.

He buttoned his waistcoat over his voluminous stomach, then put on the tailored grey jacket handed to him by one of the chartered service's beautiful flight attendants. Before disembarking, Brassington checked his appearance in the mirror hanging over the cocktail bar at the far end of the on-board lounge. He straightened his tie, and for a moment thought back to his tie-less days in the union. Brassington had been a staunch union man in Felixstowe, where he had later set up his own business, running a container yard and then opening a maritime import-export business. It was that business which had made him a very wealthy man. Yet, big Norman never forgot the old days – the days when he held a powerful grip on the industry, and dealt with union troubles efficiently, and sometimes brutally.

But times had changed. He was still physically strong, but he now wielded most of his considerable power in the boardroom, putting pressure on the opposition and squeezing his suppliers for concessions.

Brassington's luggage was briefly inspected by customs at the airport, after which he was waved through to a waiting limousine. The car took him the short distance to Marrickville, where one of his companies, Leadenhall Shipping, had acquired some land and built four storage depots and warehouses.

Upon his arrival, Jock Speller, Brassington's personal manager, collected him from the car and they walked to the nearest warehouse.

Jock had arrived in Australia the day before and sounded slightly annoyed when he spoke. "Zelda stood me up," he said, referring to Brassington's twenty three-year-old daughter. "We had an appointment scheduled yesterday."

"And you've tried the iPhone, iPad, Facetime, whatever the hell it is," said Brassington. It wasn't a question. Jock Speller was his most trusted man, and one of the most efficient people Brassington had ever met.

"The university said they hadn't heard from her in two months," said Jock.

"Sounds just like my spoilt-brat daughter," said Brassington, without emotion. "Probably fucking some playboy or, if she's anything like her mother, some homeless person."

"I'll speak to her when she surfaces," said Jock.

"Tell her I want her back at university next week or she can kiss her credit card goodbye," Brassington muttered. He had more important things to worry about, such as the Chinese importers who were muscling in on his territory. "Now tell me about Chin-fucking-Leung."

As they walked, Jock unclasped a folder from under his arm and opened it, revealing a small photograph, clipped to the page. Chin Leung was a businessman from mainland China, who had set himself up in the competitive Hong Kong markets. His export business had grown to stratospheric levels, and he blipped on to Brassington's radar when he swallowed up two of his competitors. Brassington had deep suspicions that Leung was connected to the criminal underworld, and was determined to discover his true background.

Leung was in his mid-thirties, sophisticated and, as described by Jock, "as smooth as an oil slick." He had a reputation for ruthlessness – not that it worried Brassington, given that he practically wrote the manual on ruthlessness.

"Conran Shipping has been telling me they had a meeting with Leung, about some other matter," said Jock. "Turned out it was a smokescreen. Leung was simply there to make them an offer. He has an eye on the Black Sea routes, and he's trying to undercut us – heavily."

"What did you tell them?"

"Conran? I reminded them, subtly, of the contract penalties, and told them we're in for the long haul. I told them Leung was spending big, and that it was unsustainable. It won't be long before he crashes."

"Did they believe you?"

Jock shrugged. "Doesn't matter. For the time being we've got them by the short-and-curlies. But I reckon Leung has gone for them because he knows they're our biggest client."

"So you think Leung is coming after us?"

"I'd put my pension on it."

Brassington's voice bristled when he spoke. "We're going to

dismantle this cunt, piece by piece."

Jock grinned, and opened the door to the warehouse for Brassington. They entered, unaware that they were being watched from afar. Powerful binoculars refocused automatically as the pair entered the building. There was a quiet buzz as the built-in camera snapped its final picture. The man holding the binoculars, Bernard Kemp, checked the time on his wristwatch, and slipped the binoculars into a pouch that dangled from his belt. He was standing on the fourth level of a construction site, too far away to be noticed by Brassington's security guards.

Kemp turned, made his way down a set of raw-concrete stairs to ground level, and walked to a parked Jeep. It was time to report back.

3

Jasper Owen felt an unexpected shiver running down his spine. Fear? Excitement? He wasn't sure. He was usually laid back and relaxed, especially after a day's flying and a beer or two, but now he felt edgy, nervous even.

Of course, he could just say no. But that would mean saying no to what was perhaps, as Clive Edgewood put it, a once-in-a-lifetime opportunity. He secretly wished that the decision would be made for him, so that he could stop worrying about it and simply take action.

This proposal had 'bad idea' stamped all over it, but at the same time it felt like something that might just work. On the other hand, taking the risk, even if it was small, would be stupid. Insane.

No, Jasper thought to himself. *The answer is going to have to be 'no'.* There was no other decision possible if you were a normal, logical person. Who would put up that much money for a twenty-five percent stake in a business anyway? The whole thing sounded fishy.

He shook his head, then shifted his gaze to the Blue Goose. It might not be his business, but he was doing alright: a stable job, an owner who pretty much let him take all the decisions anyway. Who wouldn't be satisfied? Jasper generally got on well with Stavros Kosta, the owner of the Blue Goose. Stavros was in his late-fifties, a man with a booming voice and a generous smile. Not someone who would retire early, Jasper reasoned. And by the time Stavros was ready, Jasper would be too. Perhaps then he could buy a stake in the business, and stay on to run the business as his own.

With the decision-making done, Jasper picked up his mobile phone and dialled the number on Clive Edgewood's business card.

Clive picked up almost immediately, much to Jasper's surprise. "Good to hear from you, pal," he said, and the line sounded crisp and clear. No phone crackle, no disturbing background noises. It was as if Clive was in a quiet place, just waiting for him to call.

"Well, yes, I had some time to think, so..." Jasper said clumsily, cursing himself for not rehearsing the conversation.

"I did a bit of phoning around, too," he heard Clive say. "Looks like your boss, Kosta, might be looking for a way out — so I'd say we timed this thing perfectly."

"*Stavros* Kosta? What do you mean a 'way out'?" said Jasper.

"He's ready to get out of the business; wants to spend more time with the kids. Isn't that great? Perfect time to set up your own business, pal."

"He... he didn't say anything like that to me."

"Of course not. He'd want to get all his ducks in a row first," said Clive.

"How... how did you—?"

"Friend of a friend," said Clive. "Turned out one of my business partners knew Stavros Kosta personally. He's a friend of the family, for God's sake. Weird, eh?"

"Yeah. Weird," Jasper agreed, the wind abruptly taken out of his sails.

"So, listen," said Clive. "I'll have a courier drop the contract off at your place tomorrow morning. After that, we're in business, buddy!" He sounded upbeat, excited.

"Yes, well, I—"

"This is your ticket, pal," he heard Clive say, though his own mind was whirling. "We'll chat tomorrow, right?"

"Ah—" Before Jasper could finish the sentence the line clicked dead.

Jasper stared blankly at the phone. It felt as if a cold hand had gripped his heart and was slowly squeezing it.

4

Stavros Kosta had two plump, bratty young sons, one aged eight and the other four. They opened the door when Jasper rang the doorbell, and immediately jostled each other, wanting to be the first to show Jasper their new toys; the latest in game controllers on which they were playing a game called 'Invasion', which put each boy in control of his own army.

"Impressive", said Jasper, eyeing the high-resolution graphics on each boy's hand-held controller.

"I won the first game," the first boy announced.

"He cheated!" shouted the second.

Jasper ignored their remarks. "Is your dad in?"

The first boy turned and shouted "Dad!" at the top of his voice. Jasper winced.

A few moments later, Jasper heard Stavros coming down the stairs. "I told you to keep those things in the play room," he said sternly to the boys, who ignored him. "You buy them one thing, they immediately want another," he complained to Jasper. "Come on, come on in," he added, gesturing for Jasper to enter. "Beer?"

Jasper shook his head.

"What's the matter? You still trying to impress that girl... what's her name?"

Jasper shook his head again. "We broke up a week ago."

"Hey Maria!" Stavros suddenly called out to his wife.

A woman's voice came from upstairs. "What?"

"Jasper's girl. She didn't work out!" Stavros shouted back.

"Aww, that's a shame," Maria replied. "Jasper, you've got to find yourself a sweet girl. Have you met my niece Stephanie?"

"You mention Stephanie every five minutes!" Stavros fired back, without allowing Jasper a moment to respond.

"She's a sweet girl," Maria's voice came back.

"Sweet," Stavros muttered. "They're all sweet, in the beginning..." He grabbed Jasper's arm and steered him into the lounge, which looked like something out of a B-grade disaster movie. Toys were strewn across the room, pillows were piled up untidily on the floor, the coffee table was turned on its side, and the sofa cushions were turned upside down. "Boys, I want you to come tidy up this place!" Stavros bellowed. The boys ignored him. "Let's go out to the pool," Stavros finally suggested.

Once they had settled into the outdoor chairs, Stavros relaxed his considerable belly so that it expanded freely and hung over his belt, and brushed a hand through his thinning, black hair. It occurred to Jasper that it seemed strange that Stavros didn't have a single grey hair, even though he was pushing his mid-fifties. Did he dye his hair? *Surely not,* Jasper thought.

"It's a good thing you popped in, Jasper," he said. "There are some things I wanted to talk to you about."

Jasper arched his eyebrows. "Same here," he admitted.

"You know what my father said? That old son-of-a-bitch, God rest his soul, always said never let an opportunity pass you by. He grew up in a little village in Greece, and he told me an opportunity was like a bus. You miss it and you may have to wait hours, maybe a whole day, for the next one. That man knew what he was talking about, I can tell you. I found that out for myself."

"What opportunity are you talking about?" Jasper queried. He was well aware of Stavros's method of adding a lot of backstory into any conversation, especially when he was about to say something that he suspected might not be well received.

"Jasper, you're like a son to me. You know that, don't you?"

"I'm a bit old to be your son, but—"

"You're like my own family. And that's why I wanted to tell you this personally, man to man, face to face."

"What are you talking about?"

"I've received offers for my businesses before, but this one... It's not every day you get such a good offer. Most of the time people try to push their luck – to see what they can get out of you. But this one? This fella has good business credentials; it's a quality offer."

"You're talking about the Goose," said Jasper.

"Maintenance costs on the Goose have been going through the roof. It's like they want your first-born, just to keep things running."

"You're selling?"

"I'm thinking about it, that's all. Just thinking. You know, with the financial trouble in Greece, I have to think of my mother;

the future," said Stavros with a pained expression.

"You said she had her own house, on a tourist island."

Stavros shrugged. "With things the way they are going – the problems with the banks – it's a mess. Who knows what they're going to do next?"

Jasper sat back in his chair, shocked at the knowledge that Stavros may have already made up his mind. "You've already decided," he said softly, his voice a mere whisper.

"It's not final," Stavros said meekly. "I'm thinking about it."

Jasper held up a hand, trying to stop his boss from explaining any further. "Stavros, there was something I wanted to ask you – the reason why I came here. And now it's even more important."

Stavros seemed surprised by Jasper's response, perhaps even slightly suspicious. "What?"

"Someone asked me to do him a favour. It's a honeymoon flight, to the islands. The man's an old friend," Jasper lied smoothly. "But he doesn't have the money for a full charter. I thought I could give him... I thought I could take him, in the Goose. Sort of a freebee, but I'm asking him to cover the fuel."

"And the insurance? What about the insurance?" Stavros wanted to know.

"But the Goose is covered. Month by month."

"I don't know, Jasper, it's a risk," said Stavros.

Jasper had had enough. "Fine," he said, rising from his chair. "I get it."

Stavros hastily stood up. "Hang on, what do you mean? What do you *get*?"

"You're just going to cut me loose, and you don't give a damn. If I hadn't turned up tonight, I wouldn't even have known about your scheme." Jasper grew angry. He felt ripped off.

"Come on," Stavros said, but Jasper turned his back and headed for the garden gate.

"Jasper, don't do this!" Stavros shouted after him. "You can have the Goose for this... trip of yours!"

Jasper paused mid-stride, and turned on the spot.

"Come on, Jasper. What are you thinking? You think I'll just turn you out in the cold? Come on, we're partners! I need you." When Jasper still hesitated, he repeated his earlier words. "You're like family to me."

"I can borrow the Goose?"

Stavros nodded, and a smile spread across his face. It was one of those smiles that begged forgiveness. Jasper hadn't seen one of those in a while.

5

Jasper flew the Blue Goose upriver, and landed near a rickety-looking jetty. A white Ford van that resembled a delivery vehicle was already waiting. From the air, Jasper had recognised Clive standing beside the van. There was another man too, presumably in attendance to give them a hand with the cargo.

Clive had suggested the handover spot. It was quiet, and they were unlikely to be seen. Only fishermen ventured this far upriver, when some of them launched their dinghies off the jetty, but at this time of year, even the fishermen were scarce because the season for river cod had not yet opened.

Jasper steered the De Havilland Twin Otter towards the jetty, then cut the engines and let it float gently until the floatplane bumped up against the jetty. He left the flight deck and stepped out on to one of the large floats, throwing a mooring line to Clive, who stood ready to receive it.

With the mooring line tied to a large wooden post, Jasper stepped on to the jetty. "Who's your friend?"

"Him?" said Clive nonchalantly. "That's Monty. He's here to look after the cargo."

"You didn't say anything about a passenger."

"I figured you could use the help on the other side. And, frankly, we could use another pair of hands here too."

Jasper could see the logic behind it, but he still felt cheated. Why hadn't Clive mentioned this person before? "Who is he?"

Clive smiled disarmingly. "He's been a friend, and associate, for many years. You have nothing to worry about. Monty's completely trustworthy."

Jasper walked with Clive towards the van. He looked Monty up and down, and noticed that the man's T-shirt spanned tightly across his barrel chest. He had day-old stubble on his chin, and eyes hidden behind reflective sunglasses. He was muscled, alright. Jasper guessed he was a military man, police, or some heavy-weight security expert.

"He spent some time in the SAS," Clive said finally. "Most people won't mess with him."

"Why isn't he in the SAS now?"

Clive smiled. "He's been discharged. Hit an officer. They said he was... unpredictable."

"A psycho?"

Clive appeared amused by Jasper's line of questioning. "Monty may have his problems, but a psychopath? No. You worry too much."

"I spent time in the air force," Jasper said. "And I know that look. That man's trouble."

"Trust me," said Clive. "If anything goes wrong, you'll be happy to have Monty at your side."

"Go wrong? What are you talking about?" Jasper was on edge, and his nervous tension was getting the better of him. "I'm thinking of calling this whole thing off."

"Come on," said Clive. "At this stage? Are you serious?"

"You set up Stavros, didn't you?"

"What?"

"You turned him on to this selling idea – just to put pressure on me."

"Don't know what you're talking about, pal." Clive's smile vanished.

"I don't trust you."

"A bit late for trust issues now," said Clive. "We made a deal, remember?"

"You mean the contract? Bet you that's some sort of bullshit too," Jasper said, his eyes flashing with anger. "This deal's off. It stinks!" Jasper turned and stomped back towards the Goose. He'd taken a good fifteen paces when an arrow struck the ground next to him, burying itself deeply in the dirt. He stopped and stared at it, then turned around slowly.

"Crossbow," said Clive. "It's Monty's speciality."

Jasper glanced across at Monty, and caught sight of the small crossbow in his hand. It had already been loaded with a second arrow. *How the hell did he do all that so quickly?*

"Maybe we should all calm down and think this over," said Clive. "What do you say?"

"So you're threatening me now?" Jasper surprised himself with his ability to display an outward calm, even though his nerve was unravelling at an alarming rate.

Clive's smile returned. "I'm a businessman, Jasper, not a thug. This is important to me. Let's be reasonable about it."

"What am I carrying? I'm pretty damn sure it's not your dead uncle," Jasper said, his voice dripping acid.

Clive maintained his smile. "We both know you never really believed that story," said Clive. "But you agreed anyway."

"Well, I'm un-agreeing."

"We have an agreement, in writing. There are penalties for pulling out. Big penalties. Come on, Jasper, you know I can't pull the plug on this now – and neither can you. Think of your future."

"At least I'll be alive in my version of the future."

Clive didn't reply immediately. When he did, he kept his voice soft, though the significance of his words cut through the morning air. "Don't bargain on it, pal."

Jasper stared at him incredulously.

Clive waited for a verbal response. When he didn't receive it, he spoke again. "By tomorrow, you'll be back here, safe and sound. And you'll have a pile of money to play with. You have my word."

Jasper still didn't respond. Panicky thoughts were flooding his brain, cutting off his ability to speak.

"Come on, Jasper. Let's do this thing."

Jasper glanced back at the Goose, before he slowly nodded.

Monty lowered his crossbow and retrieved the vehicle, driving the van up as close to the jetty as he could. He opened both the rear doors, before grabbing the handles of a raw timber box that did vaguely look like a coffin. He pulled it, and the box began to slowly slide outward. Given the way the muscles in his arms strained, it was quite heavy. Monty suddenly stopped yanking at the box and looked at Clive.

Clive joined Monty at the back of the van, then turned and spoke to Jasper. "Are you going to give us a hand?"

Jasper glanced briefly at the Goose, mentally measuring the distance between him and the floatplane. Deciding he didn't have a hope, he turned to help the two men.

Working together, they lifted the wooden box and carried it to the floatplane. The jetty creaked as they walked across it with their cargo. The Goose had two doors on the port side, one of them generally used by boarding passengers, the other for large pieces of luggage or other cargo. Jasper opened both doors, and with some heavy lifting, the three men managed to stow the box inside.

Jasper looped straps through two of the handles and strapped the box to a forward-facing bulkhead to keep it secure during the flight.

He turned to Clive. "What's in it?"

"Let's keep this need-to-know, shall we?" said Clive. "It's better for you, too, if you're ever asked to testify in future," he added with a grin.

Jasper just shook his head, and made his way to the flight deck. Behind him, he could hear Clive's voice. "Monty, I want a report-back when you land on the other side. And cut Jasper some slack. He's not in a good mood."

6

Norman Brassington held the computer-printed message in a trembling hand. Jock recognised the look of pent-up rage on his face. Big Norman's breathing was shallow, and his left hand bunched into a tight fist. His suit suddenly appeared two sizes too small for him, and his tie seemed to be strangling him.

"What do you make of it?" Norman asked in a half-choked voice.

Jock Speller didn't hesitate. "They don't mention a ransom, but you can be sure they will," he said. "This explains why we couldn't locate Zelda. I think it's genuine."

"Is it him? Is it Leung?" asked Brassington.

Speller shrugged almost imperceptibly. "He's not known for this sort of thing. But it could be that he changed tack—"

Brassington grabbed him by the forearm. "Move fast," he said. "Use the emergency fund and track this fucker. Break kneecaps. Do whatever you have to. But do it fast."

Speller nodded. "I'm sorry."

Brassington nodded an acknowledgement, then watched as Jock Speller turned and walked away.

Jock already had his mobile phone up against his ear, speaking to someone at the other end. Soon he would have a small taskforce up and running, including two detectives who were kept on twenty-four-hour retainers. Jock was undoubtedly the best man for the job – a machine of a man, who never came up with excuses, and seldom made mistakes. If anyone could track Zelda down, it was him. Brassington knew that, and yet he was deeply troubled. What if he lost the game this time? What if he lost his only daughter?

He smoothed out the note and read it again. 'We have Zelda. Instructions will follow in eight hours or less. Stand by. We don't have to tell you what will happen if you don't.'

7

Clive Edgewood played with the mobile phone in his hand. He felt its smoothness against his fingertips when he tapped the toughened glass screen. For a moment, the phone's screen sprang to life and then blinked off to blackness again.

"We must be patient," he said. "Impatience is the thing that kills a good plan."

Beside him sat a geeky young man with a dark, unruly mop of curly hair and a pair of John Lennon-style round glasses. His gaze was fixed on the computer screen in front of him.

"So I've routed us through the anonymizing servers," he said in a soft, thoughtful voice. "And the line is encrypted. So even when we're live on the call, they won't be able to track our location."

"You're a genius, Nicky. That's why I love you," said Clive with a smile. He ran his hand playfully through Nick Bennet's thick hair.

"So when are we doing it?" Nick asked. He looked a little nervous.

"About fifteen minutes before the British banks close," Clive replied. "That way, he can make that emergency call to his bank

31

manager. It adds to the pressure. Gives him less time to think. Keeps him slightly off-balance."

"It will be better to keep the call short," said Nick. "You know, just to be sure."

"Listen Nicky, I know you're nervous, but there's nothing to worry about, okay?" Clive grabbed Nick around the shoulders and gave him an affectionate hug. "Know thine enemy – that's the first rule. We know this guy's got a temper that runs hotter than a furnace. So we play on that. We get him to lose his cool… lose control."

Nick nodded, but he seemed unconvinced.

"You're going to be rich, buddy, and all for a few days' work," Clive added with a grin.

8

Jasper set a north-eastern course, reporting his position to the nearest tower. There was a storm warning for the islands to which they were heading, but he wasn't worried. It was localised bad weather, quite common in the region, and easy enough to avoid altogether.

The Goose was hitting a bit of clear-air turbulence when the flight-deck door opened and Monty entered. He didn't say a word at first, but appeared to be checking the flight deck controls.

"Can I help you?" Jasper asked sarcastically.

Monty took a crumpled piece of paper out of his pocket and handed it to Jasper. "This is where we're going," he said. His voice was gruff, unpolished.

Jasper read the coordinates and then took out a map to check the location. "Trousseau Island," he said at last. "That's where you want to go?"

Monty nodded.

"There's a harbour at the north end, but we have to get permission to land there," said Jasper, watching for a reaction.

Monty just nodded. "It's okay," he said. "It's been arranged."

"Well, I don't see how you can arrange that when—"

"It's been done," Monty cut him short.

Jasper watched him in silence for a moment. Monty was not particularly tall, but he was muscular, and it was easy to notice his wiry muscles and strong forearms. His face, too, was lean – the cheeks slightly sunken, and the eyes sharp and cold.

"Now are you going to tell me what we're carrying?" said Jasper at last.

Monty ignored the question. "I'll be back to check on you later." He left the flight deck, closing the door and leaving Jasper to his own thoughts.

9

Jock Speller sat opposite the fat man. His name was Leroy, that's all Speller knew, and he was part of a hacker network. His contact from London had put him in touch with Leroy, and the meeting was arranged within an hour.

"We don't have a name, not even a fake one," said Jock Speller. He studied Leroy's face. "It arrived by email."

Leroy leaned closer to the printed page, as if seeing the words in close-up would tell him more about the writer. Jock noticed that his face was pale, but his cheeks were a slightly rosy colour. His fine black hair was combed back and gathered in a small bun. Leroy appeared slightly bored, as if he's seen hundreds of ransom notes. When he finally spoke, his voice was soft, and had a feminine quality to it. "Neutral tone," Leroy said. "That tells us he at least knows something about playing the anonymous game. Maybe he's had some practice. But of course, we can only learn more about him once we look at the electronic signature."

"Signature?" Jock repeated.

"We follow the trail, like Sherlock," Leroy replied, offering Jock the faintest hint of a smile. "Nothing grand. We just see where the message has come from, and follow its trail back to the nearest server, then the next server, and so on. If he knows what he's doing, or thinks he does, he'll use encryption, multiple servers, onion networks, and so on."

"And...?"

"There are some we can crack, some we can't. Much depends on his level of skill, and his tools. But there's always a way to learn more. And we have good contacts..."

"When you say 'we', you mean...?"

Leroy ignored the question, opening a small laptop computer. The glow of the screen lit his face from below, giving his skin a ghoulish touch. Wordlessly, he tapped a few keys. "You've sent me the email, yeh?" he asked in the same, soft voice.

"I did," Jock confirmed.

Leroy tapped away at the keys. The screen's glow turned a greenish colour, and Jock waited patiently, while Leroy looked at reams of data scrolling down his screen. "Pretty standard stuff," he said at last. "He's trying to shield us from the host, a server in Singapore. That'll only be his first line of defence."

"Can you tell which country the original message was sent from?" Jock asked.

Leroy looked up with interest. "You know, I seldom get that question. People always assume that it's local. Only when it turns out not to be the case, do they start to look elsewhere. Is there something you want to tell me?"

"There may be," said Jock. "We have a... competitor – someone who is keen to get a slice of the pie. If there was ever a prime suspect..."

"A name would save a lot of time," Leroy announced.

"Chin Leung. Mainland China, well, most of the time anyway."

Leroy shook his head, and pondered the implications for a while. "China? Oh, man, they're keeping us busy," he muttered. "This man Leung; what can you tell me about him?" Leroy sat back in his chair, and expanded his large belly to full stretch, seemingly ready to absorb a fresh flow of information from his client.

10

Zelda Brassington was groggy from her long sleep. The drugs had not yet worn off, and her sight was foggy. The details in her vision appeared far away as she experienced a weird sense of visual distortion. Her mouth was as dry as cardboard, and she felt disorientated, but she was being dragged into the real world by force. She felt hands plucking at her clothing, roughly undoing buttons, pulling her denim shorts down, and then yanking down her panties.

Next thing she knew the man was on top of her. He had a black T-shirt on and he reeked of sweat. He was grunting, as she felt him enter her body. The act was rough and painful, and Zelda instinctively tried to push him away, but her arms felt heavy. Who was he? Where was she? She hastily tried to recollect her recent memories. At the same time, there was a noise in the background that she couldn't identify; a steady rumble of sorts. Engine noise.

The man lifted her legs up onto his shoulders, so that he could have easier access. She felt his considerable weight leaning on her, and then he thrust forward. It was violent and sudden, and Zelda yelped with pain. She tried to push him away, but her weak efforts had no effect. He was powerful, and his muscles flexed as he thrust forward, grunting aloud.

Zelda looked up and saw an aircraft window and the sunlight reflecting off it. The sun rays brightened her mind, and made her more aware of her surroundings. Her arms began to tingle as sensation returned to them, and she was aware of an extra weight to her left arm. She suddenly remembered it was a cast, placed on her arm after she broke it – an expensive, toughened plastic cast fitted at one of Sydney's elite private hospitals. She lifted her arm and stared at it, as if surprised to discover it belonged to her.

The man raping her seemed unaware that she was coming to. He was thrusting hard, his back arched and his face distorted in what appeared to be a mixture of pain and pleasure.

Zelda could see his pants discarded on the floor, along with a military-style belt with a holster, holding a Glock pistol. She groaned while staring at the pistol, but the sound was drowned out by the man's intense grunts.

The man was reaching his orgasm, his face tilted forward, and he noticed for the first time that Zelda's eyes were wide open. He frowned, but his eyes quickly lost focus as the orgasm overtook him, making his whole body shudder. He tried to lift his torso off Zelda, but before he could, Zelda had raised her arm – the one with the cast on it – and swung it at his head. The toughened-plastic cast hit him at full force on the side of the throat, and the blow caught him completely by surprise. He rolled off her, momentarily dazed by the blow.

Zelda began to crawl away from him, and she grabbed frantically at the belt and the holster. The man scrambled towards her to reach the pistol first, but he was much too late. The pistol was already in Zelda's hand, and she swung around, taking aim at him.

"Safety's on, stupid bitch!" he growled and grabbed for her.

A shot rang out, and the bullet hit his thigh. He fell backwards, hitting his head against the bulkhead with a loud thud.

Zelda rose slowly to her feet, stumbled slightly and held on to the nearest bulkhead for support. She looked at the man, lying unconscious and bleeding at her feet. "Target shooting lessons, stupid bitch." Her voice was dry, rasping.

Jasper heard the shot and hastily switched the aircraft to automatic pilot, before he hopped out of his jump-seat. Was that lunatic doing target practice on his plane? He left the flight deck to go searching for Monty.

The door to the cargo hold at the back of the aircraft was ajar, swinging on its hinges. When Jasper stepped into the cargo hold, he discovered Monty lying on the floor in a small pool of blood. The coffin, still secured against the bulkhead, was open and empty and Jasper stepped closer to investigate.

There was a narrow mattress inside the coffin, and a plastic container containing some greenish liquid, sealed with a plastic cap and fitted with a long plastic tube, presumably for sucking the liquid out. It was clear that a stowaway had been brought on board. Jasper leaned in closer to the coffin to touch the container, when he heard a voice behind him.

"Move a muscle and I'll blow your fucking head off." The voice was just loud enough to be heard above the engine noise, and held a menacing tone.

Jasper half-turned towards the voice.

"Don't move!"

Jasper realized it was a female voice and he froze. "Listen, I don't know what—"

"Shut up! On your knees!"

"I had nothing to do with this," Jasper said, not daring to make any other movement.

"If I have to ask you to get on your knees again..."

The woman was close to him now; he could sense her presence behind him.

Jasper obeyed and slowly bent down, sinking on to his knees, his hands raised to prove that he didn't intend to retaliate.

"Name?" she barked.

"I didn't even know you were aboard. I'm the pilot," Jasper explained nervously. "My name's Jasper."

"Right," she said. "You're going to tie up our friend there." The woman stepped to the side, grabbed one of the stowage straps that they used to secure random articles in the cargo hold, and threw it so that it landed at Jasper's feet.

Jasper glanced at her, and then gawked openly. She was struggling to pull up her shorts with one hand while holding the pistol in the other. She had shoulder-length brown hair, dark eyes, and beautifully smooth, tanned legs. Jasper didn't expected stowaways to be so pretty, or so dangerous.

Jasper glanced back at Monty. "He looks dead," he said anxiously. "You shot him."

"The fucker raped me," said the woman. "I don't care if he's dead. Tie him up."

Jasper picked up the strap awkwardly, uncertain what to do. He lifted Monty's shoulder, then changed his mind and tried to get the strap around Monty's feet first.

"Wait!" the woman said. "I have a better idea. Get him in the coffin."

"What? Are you serious?"

"In the coffin," she repeated. She held the pistol with more confidence now, and Jasper meekly obeyed. He grabbed Monty by the collar with one hand, his arm with the other, and pulled him slowly towards the coffin.

The woman seemed annoyed that it was taking him so long. "Bring the coffin closer, idiot!" she shouted.

Jasper glanced up at her, but didn't reply. Shaking his head, he untied the coffin from the bulkhead and dragged it over to where Monty lay. At least the coffin moved without a hitch over the metallic flooring.

When he had the coffin close enough, Jasper slipped his hands under Monty's armpits and tried to lift him. He quickly discovered Monty was a heavy load, and his body hardly budged.

"He's too heavy," Jasper complained.

"Either you get him in there, or you get in," the woman said, and she looked deadly serious.

Renewed fear clutched Jasper's stomach. He tried again, and this time managed to lift Monty's body, but only got it to the edge of the coffin. It was proving far more difficult to lift him high enough to tip him inside.

"Oh, for God's sake!" the woman said, sounding exasperated. Still holding the pistol, she helped Jasper by grabbing one of Monty's legs and lifting it high enough to add to Jasper's effort. After a few moments, Monty's body tumbled unceremoniously into the coffin. He lay face-down, and seemed as limp as before.

But Jasper thought he had noticed a slight movement. It was as if Monty was responding to the rough treatment he'd received.

"Close the lid," commanded the woman.

Jasper did as he was told, and straightened up. "I've got to get back to the cockpit. We're on autopilot and headed straight into a storm."

The woman shook her head. "Later," she said. "Right now we're dumping this coffin."

"Jesus, what are you talking about?"

"You're going to slide that coffin towards the door, and push it out."

"I can't do that," Jasper protested. "He's probably still alive! I think I saw a movement…" He pointed feebly at the coffin, shaking his head in disbelief. "Look, I don't know who you are…"

"My name is Zelda Brassington. And you're going to do exactly what I told you to do." Zelda lifted the Glock pistol to eye-height, took quick aim and squeezed off a shot. The sound was deafening in the enclosed space, and the bullet ricocheted before bursting through the fuselage, leaving behind a small hole.

"Jesus!" Jasper shouted, covering his ears and trying to protect himself with his elbows at the same time.

"I'm not going to repeat myself again," warned Zelda. "Start moving that coffin."

Jasper suddenly found a renewed burst of energy, and grabbed hold of the small handles at the front end of the coffin. He started tugging, and when the coffin finally began moving, he dragged it – slowly but forcefully – towards the cargo door.

The coffin hit an uneven section of the floor and stopped.

Jasper was forced to pull even harder, and it demanded all his strength. He paused for a moment or two, trying to catch his breath, and glanced briefly at Zelda. She was watching him without wavering, keeping the Glock aimed on him.

The aircraft bucked violently as they hit turbulence. For a moment, it seemed as if Zelda might lose her footing, but she quickly recovered and readjusted the pistol, keeping him in her sights.

"We need to find a way around the storm. If we fly straight into it, it'll break us up like matchwood," said Jasper.

"Later," Zelda barked. "Keep going."

Jasper went back to work, pulling the coffin across the floor until his back ached. He had managed to slide it out of the cargo area now, and was approaching the door.

"When we get back, I'm telling the police about this," he threatened, breathing heavily from the exertion.

"You do that," Zelda responded.

Finally, Jasper had the coffin close enough to the door. He was exhausted and sweating. The Goose was hitting a lot more turbulence, the fuselage shuddering with every new air pocket.

Jasper glanced through the porthole and saw dark-grey clouds and swirling rain. "We're losing altitude!" he warned.

"Then you'd better be quick!" Zelda shouted back.

Jasper shook his head, unable to believe the situation he found himself in. With one last, gigantic effort, he dragged the coffin all the way to the door, and then held on while the Goose bucked and shuddered. Zelda had also found a place to hold on to while she watched him.

Jasper disengaged the long handle that secured the aft door. Once the door opened at a crack, the wind came rushing in, and along with it, a fine mist. He shoved the door and it slid towards the tail. The wind was howling now, as if a hurricane had been unleashed inside the cabin.

A magazine fluttered into the air and the linen headrest covers on the seats fluttered in the air flow. The cabin floor quickly grew slick with rain, and Jasper realised he would need to step carefully to avoid falling out.

Again the Goose shuddered and dropped unexpectedly before steadying. Jasper peered out the door, and saw the ocean below them. Some of the waves crested with foam, a sign that the wind had picked up, even at sea level.

It was now or never. He grabbed the coffin handles and pushed again, as hard as he could. The coffin slid forward towards the open door. The wet slippery floor seemed to be helping.

A minute or so later, Jasper had a portion of the coffin hanging over the edge. It was then that they both heard an unmistakable thud from inside the coffin. Monty was very much alive, and was beating against the inside of the wood.

"Holy shit!" Jasper said and abruptly let go of the handles. "He's alive!"

"Push him out!" Zelda shouted.

Jasper didn't move. "He's alive!" he repeated.

Monty hammered loudly against the inside of the coffin and the noise suggested metal was being smashed against the timber lid from the inside.

"Do it!" Zelda shouted.

A crack appeared in the coffin lid. With another loud thump, the sharp point of a hunting knife protruded through the wooden lid, making Jasper jump.

"He'll kill us both!" Zelda shouted. She fired another shot

and the bullet splintered the veneered wood near the foot of the coffin.

Zelda stepped forward and shoved the pistol in Jasper's face. "Do it now, or you go with him!" she shrieked.

"Jesus!" Jasper exclaimed. He grabbed the coffin handles and pushed frantically. The coffin moved, and slid another few centimetres over the threshold.

Zelda let out a frustrated cry and pushed at the coffin with her foot. Ignoring the cast on her arm, she got onto her knees, pressing against the coffin with Jasper, the veins bulging on her neck. The coffin slowly slid forward over the wet floor, and finally tumbled out through the open doorway, freefalling swiftly to the ocean below.

Jasper and Zelda both pulled back from the open door. They were both wet and bedraggled, and their breathing was ragged and erratic.

It was the sound of one of the engines stuttering that drew Jasper's attention. "Holy shit!" he shouted. Moments later, he was flung against the bulkhead when the wing took an unexpected dip before the floatplane could automatically correct itself. Zelda moved back from the open door, and was clutching one of the passenger seats.

"Do something!" she shouted.

"This is your fault!" Jasper shouted back. "Help me get this door closed!"

Zelda tucked the Glock into the waistline of her shorts, and made her way unsteadily to the door. While Jasper pulled, she pushed. Together, they managed to get the door to close. When the door locks finally clicked into place, they were both panting from exertion.

"You killed that man!" Jasper accused, still overcome by the shock of seeing a coffin with a live human being inside it falling into the ocean.

"*We* killed him," Zelda replied. "Don't forget that."

"You forced me!" Jasper shouted, exasperated.

The Goose shook with another rush of violent turbulence, and they both had to hold on to passenger seats to avoid falling.

Jasper grabbed a life jacket from under one of the seats and threw it in Zelda's direction. "Put it on!" he shouted.

He rushed towards the flight deck, bracing himself for further turbulence every couple of steps.

11

When he opened the door to the flight deck, Jasper realised they were caught in the eye of the storm. The air currents were tossing the Goose around like a plaything, and rain lashed the foggy windshield.

He jumped into the pilot's seat, struggling to put his life jacket on simultaneously.

Using every ounce of skill and determination, he grabbed the yoke with both hands. He knew he wasn't going to be able to gain altitude, and decided to go down instead, hoping for better visibility. The battering wind that had taken control of the aircraft was forcing it towards starboard.

The Goose stabilised for a moment, but then they hit a large air pocket and Jasper felt the plane drop at stomach-wrenching speed. A flash of lightning rippled across the windshield and briefly lit up the flight deck. Jasper could hear the fuselage creaking as it was tortured by the high-velocity winds.

They were losing altitude fast. The Goose seemed determined to drop like a stone. Jasper pulled up the yoke, but it had little effect. Only one engine remained operational and it was too weak to add lift. The navigational instruments appeared to have a life of their own, and three alarms sounded simultaneously.

Jasper grabbed the radio microphone and shouted a warning to Zelda over the internal intercom system. "Get a seatbelt on! Now!"

The altimeter rotated rapidly as they descended, and Jasper noticed that their only engine was overheating, badly. He frantically peered out of the flight deck window and saw a trail of smoke coming from the engine. The next moment, it gave a final splutter and died. He was flying deadstick now, the aircraft virtually out of control and tilted at an awkward angle.

Jasper swiftly buckled himself in. Through the swirling sea mist, he could see the foamy water approaching. They were going to ditch at high speed. He battled with the yoke to try and stabilise the aircraft, and managed to lift the nose moments before the floats hit the water. The sudden impact ripped off one of the floats and the speed upended the plane on its nose. It began sinking almost immediately.

As water flooded the flight deck, Jasper opened the door to the cabin. "Get in here! We're sinking!" he shouted, and then clawed at the hatch release bracket to open the emergency escape hatch. Zelda appeared in the doorway and entered the flight deck moments before powerful jets of water began to squeeze through the opening hatch. As the hatch released, the jets became a torrent and water poured in.

They were quickly submerged. Jasper grabbed at Zelda, catching a thick mop of hair in his hand. He yanked at it, trying to swim through the open hatch simultaneously. Zelda resisted at first, but then she followed, swimming after him and grabbing on to his trouser leg.

The water's green-grey colour disappeared into darkness below, but Jasper could see the surface above him. He swam upwards with a powerful stroke of his one hand, only vaguely aware that he was dragging Zelda behind him. His lungs were already beginning to burn from the lack of oxygen, but his goal was within reach.

Moments later, he burst up through the surface, gasping deeply for air. Zelda followed. She gulped, spluttered, and then coughed as if she had inhaled some water, and beat at the water with her arms to stay afloat.

He grabbed at Zelda's life jacket and pulled the inflation cord. The life jacket inflated so swiftly that it popped and crackled, loudly enough to hear over the roar of the wind. A large wave, rimmed with foam, passed by, lifting them effortlessly in its wake. For a moment, Jasper had an opportunity to search the ocean from his heightened position. The misty rain obscured his view, but he was certain he had seen something in the distance – something that appeared to be land.

12

Nick Bennett enjoyed the weight of Clive resting against his back. The two men were naked on the bed, and Clive Edgewood had one hand curled around his lover's chest, while simultaneously kissing his neck. Nick lay face-down with his head on the pillow. He was sweaty, but satisfied.

They always enjoyed the afterglow of their energetic sexual encounters, and Clive tended to be especially tender and loving after sex, which Nick enjoyed immensely. He could feel Clive's uneven breaths on his neck, and he half-turned and smiled.

They were rudely interrupted by a continuous 'ding, ding, ding' emanating from one of the computers set up in the bedroom.

Nick raised his head, and glanced at the computer screen – the black screen had a large array of colour-coded data displayed on it. "What is that?" he said softly.

"Probably just the computer acting up. Don't fret about it Nicky," Clive said.

"No, no," replied Nick. "That's the tracker, the beacon... We've got a failure."

He wormed himself out of Clive's embrace, stood up and

hurried across to the computer, peering intently at the screen.

"I'm telling you, it's an error," Clive insisted from the bed. "They're still in the air right now." But Clive could sense his partner's unease and got up from the bed, looking a little worried.

"It's one of the most reliable... that tracker is indestructible," said Nick, suddenly cold with fear.

"Nicky, electronic gadgets act up all the time," Clive said. "You worry too much." He wrapped his hands around Nick's hips and pushed up against him playfully. His penis slipped between Nick's firm buttocks and he enjoyed the moist warmth he discovered there. His lust rekindled almost instantly.

"Dear God," Nick whispered, raw panic in his voice.

"What?" Clive peered over Nick's shoulder at the screen, which had a fluorescent green map displayed on it. A series of dots marked the passage of the floatplane, as the beacon reported its position at short intervals.

"They went off course... some time ago," said Nick. "I should have kept an eye on this."

"Cloud cover, or a storm. You know how temperamental these gadgets are," said Clive.

Nick shook his head. "They definitely went off course. A storm maybe, but the pilot would have tried to go around it." He looked up at Clive, and said in a shrill voice: "Something's gone wrong."

13

Jasper's life jacket had started slowly deflating. He had untied its cord and handed the one end to Zelda, so that she could trail behind him in the water and so that they would not be separated in the waves. The constant pull on the cord might have produced a small tear and caused the slow deflation, he reasoned. His arms felt like lead weights in the water, and he was shivering.

He glanced backwards, to ensure that Zelda was still attached. She looked tired and pale, her lips bluish with cold.

"We're drifting…" she said tiredly, her voice so weak that he could hardly hear her.

"It's alright," he replied, not bothering to explain.

After hours in the water, the land was in clear view, and they were headed in more or less the right direction, carried by a friendly current. However, they were drifting away from the spot where he had hoped they would land – a tantalising beach that he glimpsed each time the waves lifted them to a better vantage point.

It was pointless to struggle against the current, even if it was carrying them towards the rocky edge of the land mass. The rocks might be dangerous, but would certainly be a damn site better than the position in which they currently found themselves.

Summoning his remaining energy reserves, Jasper pushed on, paddling frog-like and feeling Zelda's weight dragging behind him in the water.

Then he saw it: the flash of a fin above the waterline. It appeared for just a moment, and then disappeared. Jasper stopped paddling and hung in the water, the ache in his muscles suddenly forgotten. *What the fuck was that?* His senses were alert, and his nerves raw.

"What is it?" Zelda's tired voice came from behind him.

Jasper shook his head. "Probably nothing." But then he saw it again, the top of a dorsal fin, briefly slicing through the water and then it disappeared beneath the surface. Jasper's mind was racing. If he told Zelda, she might become hysterical, something he could ill afford. But a shark? That close? It was certainly taking an interest in them.

The movement repeated and this time Zelda saw it too. "What the fuck! Is that a shark?" She sounded more alert now, and the panic was clear in her voice.

But Jasper saw something else. The flank of the animal was smooth, and light-grey. He felt perhaps he could breathe a little easier. "Maybe a dolphin," he said.

As if in reply, the dolphin broke the surface, and splashed back into the water – then took a sharp turn in their direction and swam so close that Jasper could feel the push of the water coming towards him.

Zelda screamed.

"It's definitely a dolphin!" he shouted at her. "Stay calm."

Zelda got her breath back. "What does it want?"

"It's inquisitive," Jasper replied.

"I've heard stories—" she said, and abruptly stopped, without explaining any further.

Jasper looked at her, his own face drawn with exhaustion. "What?"

"A guy who went swimming... skinny dipping, and a dolphin bit his penis."

"What the hell are you talking about?"

"Honest to God," she said.

Jasper just shook his head. "Fucking crazy," he muttered. "Forget about the dolphin. Let's get going."

"I'm exhausted," she said. "Freezing."

"You'd move faster if it was a shark," Jasper grumbled, and resumed paddling. Zelda followed him, pushing herself through the water in his wake.

It took another four hours for the two of them to make it closer to shore. Their companion dolphin disappeared occasionally, only to reappear again minutes later.

Jasper's entire body ached, and he was shivering violently. Zelda could barely move her arms, she was shaking with cold, and he'd noticed her plastered arm hanging limply in the water. Every little effort seemed to take way too much energy, a resource which was almost non-existent in supply after so long in the sea.

They drifted further northwards, and he could hear the breakers crashing against the dark, jagged rocks. The current took them slowly past a small cove, and Jasper spotted a tiny beach.

His teeth were chattering and he found it almost impossible to speak. "Must— go— there," he managed to say. He attempted to lift a weakened arm to indicate the direction. Zelda hung limply in the life-jacket. She had no energy left to move or even speak.

Jasper pulled on the cord, but her response was limited to opening her eyes. He saw that her mouth hung open limply.

"Are you alright?" Jasper said. Zelda gave a weak cough in response.

"The beach…" Jasper said. But his own words were slurred, and hardly audible. He tried to paddle forward, but his efforts had almost no effect. They were close enough to the shore now for the waves to build into larger peaks and troughs. *We need to catch just one of those waves.*

The water's motion was taking him landward, but the wave action was too weak to make much difference. Jasper attempted to kick with his legs, but his lower limbs were all but useless, hanging limply in the water.

Another wave washed past, splashing his face with water, and he choked. He was tired enough to consider sinking under the water and remaining there forever.

Jasper thought he saw the dolphin's fin appear above the waterline again, but this time it looked different, larger. It took him almost a minute to process that this was a different fin, sharper and most likely not belonging to a dolphin at all.

A large shape passed close to Jasper beneath the water, and he could sense movement very close to his legs. *"Holy shit!"* his brain screamed. He wanted to shout, but the words simply refused to come out. He saw the shark's fin again, lazily breaking the surface and then gliding along smoothly. *Was the bloody thing curious about them? Sizing them up?*

Jasper's legs tingled, and kicked back into life. Seeing the shark had jolted his worn-out nervous system into action. He kicked with both legs, and moved himself through the water, still dragging Zelda along with him. Frantically, he started grabbing handfuls of water, clawing his way forward – towards the land.

Splashing desperately, he found himself helped along by a small wave that pushed both of them along for a few more metres, before it left them bobbing on the surface.

"A shark…" Jasper managed to say. "I saw a shark."

Zelda hung limply in the water. She didn't respond, and Jasper was beginning to think she hadn't heard him when she spoke. "What?" Her voice was very weak and croaky.

Jasper drew a deep breath when he noticed that behind Zelda, a large wave was building.

He lifted one hand to warn Zelda, but the wave was already upon them, foaming angrily at its lip. They were swept up in a wall of water, and carried forward at speed, in a demented surfing streak, for a few metres before being unceremoniously dumped again.

Jasper went under in a swirl of white-water, fine sand and millions of air bubbles. His elbow struck the sand below. Instinctively, he planted his feet in the sand at the bottom, then kicked away and swam for the surface.

Surprised at his own strength, he broke well clear of the surface – and immediately noticed the beach was closer now. He glanced around frantically, but Zelda was nowhere to be seen. Another wave approached and Jasper took a deep breath and dove under it, half-expecting to see her body drifting lifelessly beneath the water. There was no sign of her.

Puzzled, he resurfaced. But then he spotted movement on the water. Zelda was closer to the beach than he was, and she was swimming for the shore. Jasper was surprised to see that she had recovered so swiftly. He began swimming in the same direction.

He spotted the dark shape in the water again, and as if to confirm his fears, an angular fin cleaved the water about twenty metres away. The shark had not given up. Jasper remembered seeing nature documentaries on TV, in which sharks not only swam in the surf but sometimes partially beached themselves in the pursuit of prey. He tried to blot those thoughts out of his mind, and pushed on, swimming steadily, but with arms so tired that they ached unbearably.

The shark circled, and Jasper turned towards it, waiting anxiously for an attack. He desperately tried to recall the advice of shark experts about what to do when faced with an imminent shark attack. *Poke the eyes. Wasn't that what they recommended?*

Again, the shark disappeared from view, and Jasper resumed his efforts to reach the beach. Zelda was on the beach, staggering to her feet, falling down again, and finally lying motionless on the sand.

Jasper redoubled his efforts. *If she could make it...*

The shark appeared right beside him. With his face half-submerged, Jasper could see it was heading straight for him. He twisted his body, and pushed away with his arms and legs, before the tough, leathery skin touch his. Instinctively hitting out to protect himself, he managed to a glancing blow off the shark's flank – and it reacted immediately, darting away from him.

He now knew two things. The shark was larger than he had thought, and it had supreme agility in the water.

Jasper was overcome with panic, and he powered forward, swimming with large strokes, his hands clawing desperately at the water.

A sudden wave lifted him, and Jasper instinctively tucked his elbows into his sides, streamlining his body – just as he had when body-surfing as a teenager. The wave's momentum carried him forward, and he picked up speed. The wave was enormous, and he was near its crest, driving forward at a thrilling speed. White-water foamed around him as the wave began to break, but still it carried him, further and further onwards. For those few moments, Jasper's fears melted away, and he was only aware of the breathtaking power of nature that swept him along.

He found himself in far shallower water – so much shallower that he could feel the sand beneath his feet. Stumbling, trying to scramble out of the water at the same time, Jasper looked over his shoulder, expecting the shark to reappear.

But it didn't.

Jasper waded ashore, his legs threatening to buckle beneath his weight. He finally made it onto the beach, where he collapsed on his knees. He crawled forward, still driven by fear of the shark. Finally confident he was far enough from the water, he fell down flat on the sand, exhausted and gasping for air.

He lay there for several minutes, unable to move even a muscle.

Then he thought about Zelda. *Where was she?*

14

Norman Brassington leaned forward in the office chair, mobile phone pressed hard up against his ear, and listened intently to the voice at the other end.

"I was told this is the best number to get you on," the voice said.

The little hairs at the back of Brassington's neck stood erect. He realised instantly that he was talking to the kidnapper.

"Where did you get this number?" he asked, trying to put a casual tone into his question. It didn't convince Clive, whose emotional antennae were alive and picking up every nuance.

"You know what this is about," Clive said simply, giving Brassington some time and allowing the confirmation to sink in.

"I... do," said Brassington after a pause. He noticed a tiny echo as he spoke, and a distinct flatness in the voice at the other end. *No doubt some electronic trickery to disguise the number and the identity of the caller,* he thought, and wished that Jock was on hand to listen in on the conversation.

"I'll keep this simple," Clive said. "You will receive the instructions in another email. Don't bother tracking it – that will be a waste of your time. You will follow the instructions to the letter. Doing anything else will prove to me that you have no interest in... participating. That will put an end to our conversation, and I will never contact you again. Do you understand?"

"I will need proof," said Brassington.

"You will get none. You will simply follow my instructions." Clive's voice was calm, controlled.

"Listen, you fucker. I want proof that my daughter is well!" Brassington broke out of his controlled shell. His voice turned to a growl. He was spitting venom.

"You'll need time to think about this," Clive replied, his voice dead calm. "Consider the situation you are in."

"I will take your fucking skin off and feed it to you, you miserable scum!"

It was quiet at the other end for a moment, then Clive's voice broke through the silence. "It was fun chatting. Must go now."

"I will track you down if it's the last thing I do on this earth," Brassington said, his voice a touch quieter now, but glowing with the fires of hell.

The voice at the other end cut off, and the call terminated.

Brassington rose from his chair, grabbed the large desk with both hands and flipped it over with such force, it bounced and one of the legs broke off. He was unable to speak, only managing growling noises like a wounded bear. His large hands were bunched into tight fists, and it took gigantic effort to regain control of his anger.

The mobile phone, which had landed on the floor, suddenly beeped quietly and the screen lit up. It was Jock.

15

Beach sand clung to Jasper's body when he stood up. He glanced back at the water, and began following the footprints in the sand. Zelda's footprints led to a sandy stretch between two trees, which looked like a natural path. After that, they disappeared.

Jasper was still shivering, and he imagined Zelda would be too. It was clear that Zelda didn't trust him. Jasper shook his head involuntarily. Was she really convinced that he was in cahoots with the kidnappers? The thought made him refocus on Clive. *That two-timing bastard.*

Jasper felt the anger boil inside him. In a way, it was helpful, because it gave him renewed energy to go on. He wanted to search for Zelda; explain everything. But the situation in which he found himself was simply absurd. He didn't know exactly which island they were on, nor could he tell how big it was or if anyone else was living on it.

What if people *were* living there and Zelda reached them before he had the chance to explain himself? If they heard her story first, they'd lock him up without a moment's hesitation — Jasper was sure of it. He trudged on, watching for the tiniest movement and listening for any tell-tale noises which might point him in the right direction.

After about twenty minutes, he stopped walking. What if he'd already passed by her without realising it? Jasper studied the sky. He didn't wear a wristwatch and his mobile phone was at the bottom of the ocean, so it was difficult to guess the time. He estimated that it was late afternoon, probably four or five o'clock. In that case, he reasoned, there wasn't much daylight left. He'd have to find shelter, and if he was lucky, something to eat.

The search for shelter took about forty-five minutes. Jasper found a rock overhanging a sandy patch on one of the hills. The sand was slightly hollowed out and gave the impression of a reasonably comfortable outdoor bed. *So far, so good.*

The hunt for food took longer. Jasper found a cluster of mussels on the rocks, but the restless waves made an approach somewhat risky. However, it appeared as if the tide could be going out. Jasper could scarcely believe his luck. All he needed to do was wait, and a bounty of mussels could be his for the taking.

But then he heard Zelda's voice behind him.

"You'd better not make one wrong fuckin' move," she said. The harsh tone in her voice suggested she was deadly serious.

Jasper turned to face her, and saw the pistol in her hand. "You carried that heavy thing with you? It's no wonder you almost drowned. I thought you'd—"

"Shut up!" It seemed Zelda was in no mood for chit-chat. "I want you to explain to me exactly what this clusterfuck was about."

"Listen…" Jasper began hesitantly, his eyes locked on the weapon. "We survived – against freakin' astronomical odds. So why don't we make peace, and I'll tell you everything you want to know – everything I know, anyway."

"You tell me everything right fucking now," she replied, her mouth twitching with anger.

"Fine, fine. Alright," said Jasper. "I'm a pilot... charter flights, mostly. So I got a call from this guy, Clive. His last name was..." for a panicky moment, Jasper couldn't remember it. Then he said: "Edgewood, that's his name."

Zelda nodded slowly, encouraging him to continue.

"He said he wanted to fly a body – his uncle who had died – to the islands. Only, there was some legal problem in getting the body out. Something about the uncle being in jail for years. I told him the whole thing sounded pretty damn fishy and that I wanted nothing to do with it."

"And?"

"That's when he started telling me how low the risk was, how much money he would pay, and that he could easily find someone else if I didn't take the opportunity."

"And you believed him?"

Jasper wavered. "Well, he also suggested the chartering business I was working for was on the way out. Of course I didn't believe him. Things were going pretty okay, I thought. But then I had a chat with the owner of the charter business; my boss. And he kind of suggested that he was looking at selling. He didn't say anything about that before, ever."

"And that's what got you to take the deal?"

Jasper suspected he looked like a dog that had been caught eating the evening roast. "Kind of."

"And what was the Neanderthal doing on the flight?" Zelda asked sharply.

"The man we... pushed out?"

Zelda rolled her eyes. "Who do you think?"

"His name was Monty. That's all I know. He turned up this morning. He was never part of the arrangement..." Jasper voice trailed off. He wasn't sure how much of his story sounded even remotely believable.

Zelda appeared to be in deep thought for a moment. Then she asked: "How much? How much did he pay you?"

"To date? Nothing. Not yet."

"You were going to do all this illegal shit and you didn't ask for a deposit?"

Jasper shrugged slightly. "We have a contract. He signed a contract."

"And how's that working out for you?"

"Listen, if you didn't force me to fly into a storm—"

"Me? Oh, so it's all my fault, is it? If all else fails, blame the fucking kidnap victim!"

"That's not what I—"

"Jesus, you must be a moron!" Zelda shouted in frustration. "A fucking blind man would have seen that coming." Zelda shook her head. "I always thought, you know, that pilots had a little something... up here." She tapped her finger against her scalp. "But you... Jesus!"

"I know you're angry—" Jasper started, but he was quickly cut short.

"I'm fucking livid, man! What do you think?" Zelda exploded. "Kidnapped by a conman, raped by a Neanderthal and stuck on an island with a fucking moron! How do you think I feel?"

Jasper thought it wiser not to answer her question.

16

The motor yacht gleamed in the sunlight. Chrome trim and a wood-panelled aft deck gave it the look and feel of ultimate luxury.

"She's got twin eighty-horsepower engines to keep you purring along nicely," the man from the Manacca Luxury Boat Hire Company told Clive Edgewood, gently running his hand over the instrument console. "We can supply a skipper if you need one."

Clive shook his head, but he was impressed with the exterior. "So tell me Winston, will she handle some rough weather?" he asked with a warm smile.

"Absolutely. Where were you thinking of cruising to?"

Clive shrugged, as if he still needed to make up his mind about his course. "Here and there," he said, "but I'd rather be safe than sorry."

"I know exactly what you mean, sir. This one's got an excellent safety rating – reinforced hull, and excellent sea-handling. But of course, she offers plenty of comfort, too."

"Now let's say I'm a little... impatient. What sort of performance can I expect?" asked Clive.

Winston had the information at his fingertips. "In perfect conditions, it's possible to push her all the way up to thirty five knots – but of course, conditions aren't always perfect..."

Clive nodded. "Range?"

"About four hundred and fifty kilometres," Winston replied, "again depending on conditions." Then he changed tack. "Why don't I show you down below?"

"Please do," Clive agreed, and he followed Winston down the steps to the cabin.

Veneered wood panels and thick luxury carpeting enveloped them below decks. The motor yacht was beautifully fitted out. A surprisingly roomy head and a main cabin with large double bed impressed Clive. He sat on the edge of the bed and sighed.

"I could live here," he said.

"It's a dream isn't it?" said Winston, who appeared to enjoy his job.

Clive stared at him curiously for a moment. "I bet it's a pretty good spot to have a party," he suggested.

Winston turned to him and smiled. "You can say that again. I've been to few parties on board these babies." He looked slightly bashful when he noticed Clive was staring at him.

Clive stood up and touched his shoulder. "If I have a party on board, you can consider yourself invited," he said with a smile, lightly resting a hand on Winston's shoulder before sliding it down to his upper arm.

Winston glanced at his hand, but didn't pull away.

"I forgot to mention that we stock the fridge with a couple of bottles of excellent champagne," Winston said, matching Clive's smile.

"If I agree to sign up for the charter, can we taste some now?" Clive gazed into the younger man's eyes and instantly recognised a spark of excitement, anticipation flaring in his irises.

"I can't see why not," Winston responded.

Clive slipped his hand behind Winston's neck and gently pulled him closer. He noticed that Winston's lips had parted a little, and the younger man was trembling slightly.

"Will we have some privacy here?" he asked.

Winston nodded, and Clive pulled him closer and kissed him deeply.

17

Jasper had waded into the water and was picking mussels off the rocks while Zelda watched his every move, the pistol still clutched in her hand.

He had his shirt folded up and used it as a basket to store his pickings. "These are okay to eat raw. They're not bad," he said.

Zelda merely grunted in response.

"Hey, there're some oysters here too!" he called out excitedly.

"Stay where I can see you!" Zelda shouted back, pointing at him with the pistol.

Jasper shook his head at her. "Relax, will you? Do you honestly think I'll run for it? On this island?"

"Stay where I can see you," Zelda repeated.

Jasper shrugged and turned his attention to prising open an oyster, but found it remained stubbornly sealed. He tried a different oyster, but the result was the same. "If only I had a knife..." he muttered.

"Well you don't, genius."

Jasper glanced up at her. "Are you always this ratty?"

Zelda grimaced, but didn't reply.

He eventually waded back and brought his booty ashore, depositing the mussels and oysters on to a flat rock. "People pay good money for this in the city," he said proudly.

"They're raw," Zelda complained.

"They're fresh," Jasper countered. It took some effort to crack open the first mussel, using a stone. He tried a mouthful, chewing enthusiastically. "Tastes like seawater," he finally announced.

"Now there's a surprise," Zelda replied dryly. She looked exhausted.

"Want to try one?"

Zelda wrinkled her nose and shook her head firmly.

"If only..." Jasper said, surveying the area around him. "...If only we had something to cook them in."

Zelda didn't bother replying. She stood up, tucked the pistol into her shorts, turned and began walking away from the beach.

"Where are you going?" Jasper shouted after her.

"I need some sleep. Somewhere dry," she replied.

"I've already found a good spot," he said.

But Zelda continued walking without pause. "I advise you to stay away from me," she said.

"You're not worried about me running away anymore?"

Zelda carried on walking, and he could hear her mutter. "I don't give a fuck."

Jasper shrugged, and shook his head. "Your loss," he said softly, and picked up another mussel, breaking the hard shell to retrieve the meat inside. *Maybe this wasn't so bad after all.*

Free seafood. A tropical beach. Company could be better though. He tucked into the second mussel, and somehow it tasted a little better than the first.

While he enjoyed his meal, he stared out at the ocean, his gaze fixed on the distant horizon. *Would anyone come for them?* Jasper realised they had flown far off course, and the current would have washed them even further from their planned route. On the other hand, there weren't that many unknown, deserted islands. There was bound to be a fishing vessel, or maybe even a cruise ship passing by at some stage, he reasoned.

To survive they would simply need shelter, a reasonable food supply, and drinkable water. The thought of water suddenly filled his mind with panicky thoughts. What if there wasn't a drop of fresh water on the island? They might have to rely on rain – but what if it didn't rain?

It occurred to Jasper that it would be wise to start the search for fresh water straight away, and a higher vantage point would help him find it faster. With that thought in mind, he walked along the beach, searching for natural pathways to higher ground. In many places, rocks prevented an easy ascent, but then he spotted what looked like a sandy path cutting between the trees.

As Jasper approached, he noticed a shiny object on the sand, and then another. It certainly wasn't the virgin beach he had earlier imagined. The shiny objects were discarded beer cans, bleached by sun exposure, their metallic surfaces reflecting the sunlight.

Between the trees was a flattened sandy patch, and evidence of an old campfire. He found more rubbish strewn around the area; empty plastic bottles, a fork with all its teeth bent, rusted food cans, and even part of a torn shirt, half-buried in the sand. His eye caught another shiny object, glistening in the sun –

a shell from a spent ammunition cartridge. Jasper bent down and picked it up, holding it thoughtfully in his hand. As a pilot, he had heard that smugglers were known to use some of the islands in the region as hide-outs. The picnickers were clearly armed – not exactly the kind of rescue party he'd had in mind.

18

Jock Speller pulled up in front of what appeared to be a construction site near the ocean. The building still had a sign proclaiming 'Beach Retreat' attached to its front facade, but the sign had grown old and faded with the passage of time. It was apparent that the building was in the process of being refurbished. Large sheets of tough, industrial-strength clear plastic covered most of the windows, and scaffolding had been erected against several of the outside walls.

Jock located a set of stairs, covered in concrete dust, and walked to the entrance. The door was barred and emblazoned with a sticker that read 'Construction site. Authorised personnel only'. He went in search of an alternative entrance and found a side door open, and could immediately smell fresh plasterwork and paint from inside.

Leroy sat at a little table near one of the windows, his attention focused on a laptop computer screen. He glanced up as Jock approached, and gestured for him to sit down.

Jock hung his jacket over the back of the chair and settled onto it, watching Leroy as he tapped lightly on the keys. He noticed a small plastic container next to Leroy's computer. As he watched, Leroy removed the lid with one hand and continued to scan the contents of the small screen. The opened container was filled with chopped carrots. Leroy scooped up a handful and put them in his mouth, chewing loudly.

"Cholesterol," he announced. "Doctor said I should eat more raw veg."

Jock nodded.

"So you work for Norman Brassington," Leroy said casually.

Jock nodded again. He knew it was only a matter of time before Leroy checked into his own background. "You said you had made some progress," he said. He wanted to avoid divulging any information about Norman Brassington if it were possible.

Leroy tore his gaze from the screen, and studied Jock briefly. "The thing is, most people think they can disappear on the 'net," he said. "They can disappear temporarily, but in the end, they always slip up and make a mistake. There's always little clues left behind."

Jock leaned forward in interest.

"We haven't got him yet, but there are some clear markers. He's here. He's a local boy. He's tried his best to mask IP addresses, but they're always routed back here, in one way or another." He grinned briefly. "That'll make it easier."

"So you think you'll track him down?"

Leroy appeared confident. "It's just a matter of time."

"There is an... urgency involved," said Jock.

"I get that," said Leroy. "We don't want to disappoint our customers."

Jock nodded. He surveyed the interior of the room where they sat. "What is this place?"

Leroy smiled. "A hotel, once upon a time. A friend of a friend told me they were renovating it. Thought it was a good spot to meet."

"It is," said Jock. "When can I expect—"

"Results? Very soon now. We've got some good leads and I've got an expert working on it."

"Sounds promising," said Jock as he got to his feet.

"Our phase one payment..." Leroy began. "That's due now."

Jock nodded. "I'll make sure it happens."

"You're a gentleman," Leroy said with a satisfied nod. He didn't bother getting up, but watched Jock as he let himself out.

19

Clive unsheathed a long diving knife and stared at the twenty-centimetre blade. "Just look at this baby," he said, admiring the weapon. The rubberised handle was thick and comfortable in his hand.

Nick Bennett stared at him, clearly agitated. "You can't just leave all this shit up to me," he said angrily.

Clive's voice was calm, his tone even. "We've got a situation here," he said. "You know that."

Nick slumped down in front of his computer and stared at the screen.

Clive moved closer and touched Nick's slender neck. Nick shook his head determinedly and grabbed Clive's hand, forcefully pushing it away. Clive was taken aback by Nick's fierce reaction.

"He phoned..." Nick said.

"Who?"

"You *know* who. The guy... from the charter company."

Clive lifted an eyebrow. "Wait, did I do something wrong?"

"I don't know. Did you?" Nick's tone was sharp.

"So that's what this is about? You suspect I—"

"Don't lie to me," Nick cut in. "Don't you dare fucking lie to me."

"I don't even know what you're talking about," Clive lied.

"I could hear it in his voice! You two are pretty comfortable aren't you? And I looked him up online. Winston. Pretty boy. Just your type."

"Oh, come on, Nick," Clive said, feigning complete innocence. "There was nothing between us. This is crazy."

"You've got the boat," Nick said. "He's sending the contract."

"Well, that's great."

"Just perfect," said Nick sarcastically. "Is he going with you? Is he the… skipper?"

"What are you talking about? Of course not. It's business. *You* know that."

"And fucking him? Was that business?"

"Nick, I swear to you. Nothing happened."

"You lie," said Nick, his eyes teary. "You do nothing but lie."

"Nick," said Clive slowly. "I need you to pull yourself together. We have a situation here, and I'm trying to fix it."

"Tell me the truth," Nick demanded.

"I need this boat. I need to find out what happened. I have to go there myself – you know that!"

"Tell me the truth!"

Clive held up his hands in defence. "There's nothing to tell, I swear to you."

"Then swear it on his life. Swear it on your mother's life!"

"You're hysterical," Clive said softly.

Nick leapt from his chair and fled to the bathroom.

Clive followed, but found the bathroom door locked. Inside, he could hear Nick sobbing.

"Nick..." he said and listened. No reply. "Nick I need you, now more than ever. Do you hear me?"

Still no reply.

"Remember what I promised you?" said Clive. "When this is over, it's you and me. Only the two of us. We put all this behind us and we fly to paradise."

The sobbing had stopped, but there was no other response from the other side of the door.

"I promise you, Nick. I promise on my dear mother's life..." Clive stood quietly and waited. Then he whispered: "Just you and me."

A full two minutes passed, before the bathroom lock clicked open.

20

Cigar smoke hung mid-air in the plush hotel suite. The spacious bedroom extended into a separate, attractively-decorated lounge where a large painting dominated one of the walls.

Norman Brassington's bulky body sank into the couch, and he sighed deeply. Jock Speller stood and watched him, waiting for a signal that this was a good time to discuss the 'project'. Brassington gestured absent-mindedly towards one of the armchairs, and loosened another of the top buttons on his shirt.

Jock sat down and opened his briefcase, extracting a thin manila folder. "Would you like to see this?"

Brassington stared at him, taking out a handkerchief to mop his sweaty forehead. "Will it mean anything to me?"

"Not much," Jock replied.

"So what about my money? Are we pissing it away on useless information?" Brassington said aggressively.

"In my opinion, no," Jock replied. He opened the manila folder and glanced at the contents, before he looked up at Brassington again. "I know you're edgy, but these people are getting closer. A bit more time, and—"

"For all I know, Zelda is already dead," Brassington announced bluntly, and immediately regretted his words. He had wanted to keep his own hope alive, and his current mood wasn't helping.

"I'm sorry, Norm. If I had a better plan…"

Brassington shook his head, waving his hand in a feeble attempt to retract the words he'd uttered.

"The kidnappers are using several methods to disguise their identity and whereabouts online," Jock said, searching for simple words to explain the problem. "It's not easy to crack it, but they are having some success."

Brassington nodded. "How long?"

"Twenty-four hours, maybe. They listen for online chatter, and analyse it. Every clue gets them closer."

"I hope these fucking computer geeks aren't screwing us. Because I'll tell you…" Brassington dropped his intended threat mid-sentence, his hand balled into a tight fist.

"Have you eaten something?" Jock asked, with genuine concern.

Brassington shook his head.

Jock stood up. "I'll get you some room service," he said, and readied himself to leave.

"Jock," Brassington said. "Get these fuckers. I want you to track them down. I've been screwed many times in my life, but this time…"

Brassington's deep voice sounded fragile, and Jock gazed at him sympathetically. "Whatever I can do," said Jock. "I won't stop until we get them."

Brassington nodded slowly, leaning back on the couch and closing his eyes.

Jock left the hotel suite and quietly closed the door behind him.

21

Zelda was awoken by an ache in her arm. It was as if the cast had dried and then tightened, constricting the blood flow. It was a state-of-the art plasticised cast, sturdy yet light-weight, but obviously not designed for people stranded on tropical islands, she thought sourly. Still, it had its uses – such as fighting off rapists, for instance.

The broken radial bone was the result of a drunken stumble after an all-night party with friends – something Zelda still regretted.

She sat up, sand clinging to her side and her hair. She shook her head a few times and breathed deeply in the fresh sea air. For a few moments, she toyed with the idea of getting rid of the cast altogether – but the thought of removing it without being certain the bones had fully knitted made her nervous. *Besides,* she thought, *the cast provided a convenient hiding place.*

She probed beneath the outer layer of the cast, digging deeper with her fingers until she found what she was looking for – the edge of a credit card. She pulled it out with a pincer-like movement of her fingertips, and stared at its smooth, glossy surface. It was an exclusive black credit card, which allowed its owner to withdraw large sums of cash and undertake no-questions-asked transactions anywhere in the world. It was imprinted with her name 'Zelda Brassington' in dark-platinum letters. Owning one of these cards was a perk that came from being the daughter of a businessman who regularly found himself on Britain's 'richest men' lists.

The pin number for the card was so long and difficult to remember, Zelda had stupidly decided to scratch the numbers on the underside of the cast. Now, it was impossible to erase.

She was about to rise to her feet when warm droplets of liquid fell on her bare arm. She looked upwards and squinted when more of the droplets fell from somewhere above. *Warm water?* It didn't make sense.

Zelda stepped back and examined the hill above her. On a ledge a few metres higher, she saw Jasper, taking a piss.

"What the fuck!" she shouted.

"Holy shit!" she heard him cry out. "I didn't know you were down there!"

"You pissed on me, arsehole!"

"I'm sorry. I swear I didn't—"

"You have the entire island to piss on, and you pick this spot! What do you take me for? A fucking moron?" Zelda's voice was fibrillating with rage.

"I promise you..." Jasper tried again. "I promise, I didn't know!"

Zelda mumbled a few more expletives, and stomped off in the direction of the ocean. As she walked, she ripped off her T-shirt. Reaching the water's edge, she dropped the pistol onto her discarded T-shirt, and removed every other piece of clothing. She waded into the water, splashing water over her arm and body and scrubbing her skin clean.

"I'm sorry," Jasper muttered again, but she was too far away to hear him. He couldn't keep his eyes off Zelda as she washed in the knee-deep water. He found himself appreciating the view of her body, and was surprised by her sensuality, even during a fit of anger.

Her dark hair was beautiful, shimmering in glossy waves in the sunlight. Jasper's mouth grew dry, and he knew he was intruding on her privacy, but found it impossible to tear his eyes away. A split-second passed, before he noticed there was something else in the water – a dark shape moving swiftly in Zelda's direction. The shark was back.

"Holy shit!" he exclaimed. In the next instant he was running down the hill towards the water's edge. "Get out!" he screamed. "Get out of the water!"

Zelda looked up and wiped her hair back from her face. A demented-looking Jasper was running towards her at full tilt, waving his arms frantically in the air.

Her first thought was that Jasper was heading for the pistol – to grab it before she had the opportunity to retrieve it. "Son of a bitch!" she shouted and scrambled for the shore.

Zelda found herself slightly ahead in the crazy race. She used all her energy to power forward, then ran up onto the beach and dove for the pistol, fumbling for a moment before she managed to grab it in her right hand, and level it at Jasper.

Jasper's breath was rasping in his throat. "There was…" he gasped between deep breaths, "there… a shark."

Zelda was also exhausted and breathing heavily. "You've got to be fucking kidding me," she said tiredly.

She stumbled to her feet, still pointing the pistol at Jasper.

"Step away," she demanded.

"What?" Jasper was incredulous. "There was a shark, coming for you in the water. Don't you—?"

"I'm about two seconds away from shooting you in the head, arsehole," Zelda growled.

"For God's sake, look! Look for yourself!" he said, pointing at the water. He found that despite the bizarre circumstances they found themselves in, he couldn't help casting another admiring glance over Zelda's naked body.

"Step away! I'm not telling you again," she said.

Jasper stepped backwards, raising his hands defensively. "Take a look for yourself..." he demanded.

When he was at a safe distance, Zelda glanced over at the water. There was no sign of any shark. When she turned back, Jasper's gaze had drifted down to her buttocks, but he quickly looked away towards the ocean.

Zelda lifted the pistol and carefully aimed at Jasper's forehead.

"What? What are you doing?" he asked, stepping back even further.

Zelda's hand was trembling, but she managed to hold her aim. "You try a stunt like that again, and I will kill you," she said, her voice low and menacing.

"I swear to you—"

"Shut up!" Zelda snapped. "One more time, and I will shoot you like a dog."

"I know you don't believe me," he tried again, but Zelda held up a hand to stop him.

"I'm hungry, tired, and..." she glanced down at her own body, "...naked. And I want you to go away."

Jasper nodded, and took another step in retreat, but remained facing her. "I was trying to help," he said. "That's all." He turned around and slowly began walking away, glancing over his shoulder once or twice, half-expecting Zelda to tell him to stay. But she didn't.

Zelda finally lowered the pistol to her side, and sighed deeply. Extreme fatigue had crept into her bones, and she was ready to burst into tears. Everything seemed so hopeless.

She turned around to retrieve her clothes from the sand and brushed them off. When she looked up, she noticed movement in the water, beyond the breakers. It was unmistakable: a shark's dorsal fin cleaved the water, and Zelda watched in shock as it swam around lazily.

"Shit," she whispered.

22

Luxury yachts lined the jetties at one of the most upmarket yacht clubs Bernard Kemp had ever seen. It was warm enough to wear a T-shirt, and a pair of shorts with large pockets on the sides, but he felt distinctly underdressed. Well-fed, elderly men approached their boats wearing cream trousers and navy blazers, some of them sporting baseball-style caps to add a touch of informality.

Bernard placed his canvas-style duffel bag by his feet. It contained all the essentials: spare T-shirts and jeans, polar fleece tops, basic toiletries, underwear and socks, a cap, sunscreen, mosquito repellent, a quarter bottle of brandy, rigging gloves in case he needed them, and rubber-soled shoes for working on the deck in wet conditions. He had also chucked in a pair of Hawaiian-patterned board shorts as an afterthought. Concealed at the bottom of the bag was his more precious luggage: a dismantled RSASS sniper rifle with telescopic sights and a hundred rounds of ammunition, a hunting knife with serrated blade in a heavy duty, rubberised sheath and a stainless steel revolver, fully loaded and with 50 rounds of ammunition stored in two plastic, sealed containers.

The weapons were unlicensed and highly illegal in Australian territorial waters, but Bernard knew there were plenty of hiding spots on a large motor yacht, and authorities were less likely to check luxury craft, especially in an exclusive club like this one. He lifted a pair of high-powered binoculars to his eyes and peered at several of the moored boats, casually watching the coming and going of the 'boaties'. Several of them were ageing, plump boat owners, along with assorted hangers-on – curly-haired, leanly-muscled boat hands, bikini-bottomed and honey-tanned twenty-something-year-old women, and the occasional trophy wives, well past their use-by date, their skins leathered from overexposure to the sun.

He panned the binoculars towards the clubhouse, and saw Clive's Mercedes Benz in the parking lot. *Not long now,* he thought, and sniffed the fresh sea air with a smile.

Clive approached, wheeling a large suitcase, and carrying a smaller bag over one shoulder. He smiled, confidently as always. Bernard nodded in acknowledgement, and put his binoculars back in the black pouch which was attached to his belt.

"Good day for it!" shouted Clive when he was within earshot.

Bernard nodded. "Are we clear to go?"

"You betcha." Clive approached the gangplank that had been set up to welcome them aboard *Silver Tambourine* – all the Manacca Luxury Boat Hire Company's vessels carried names of musical instruments. "Give me a hand, will you?" He paused for a moment until Bernard took the larger suitcase from him, and carried it across the narrow gangplank.

They took the luggage below, and Bernard was quietly impressed with the luxurious vessel.

Clive saw his admiring glances and spoke up. "Cost a pretty penny, but this baby is going to get us there in a hurry," he said.

"So you know where 'there' is?" Bernard said doubtfully. He considered himself a healthy sceptic.

Clive nodded. "We know where the plane disappeared off the map, the direction of the current, where the nearby islands are located. We'll be alright." He paused and looked Bernard up and down. "You're ready for this?"

Bernard nodded. "Been ready since yesterday."

"Good." Clive smiled. "Let's cast off."

23

The flight from London to Sydney ran about twenty minutes late – not bad for an international flight that had a stop-over *en route*. Even though it was late-evening, the airport arrivals lounge was buzzing, and passengers arriving from overseas waited patiently in line to have their passports checked, before proceeding to the customs hall.

Three men, all of them sporting brush-cut hair and tanned skin despite the dreadful London weather, stood quietly in the queue. They wore plain and comfortable clothes; jeans, T-shirts, light jackets, and running shoes – and it was easy to see all three were in prime physical shape, as if they had spent hours training in the gym.

They stood in different queues, trying to blend in with groups of tourists and returning locals – some of them families – exasperated by the long flights and trying to calm their unruly kids.

The first of the three men reached the counter. A man sat behind it at a small partitioned desk, a passport scanner mounted in front of him. He appeared tired after a long shift, and eyed each new passenger with the same, slightly suspicious gaze.

"Passport," the immigration official requested without enthusiasm. He was slightly resentful about a passenger appearing so alert after such a long flight. The passenger passed his passport over the counter, immigration card tucked inside.

"The reason for your visit?" the immigration official asked.

"Holiday," the passenger responded.

"Do you have any relatives living in Australia?"

The passenger shook his head. "None."

The man's passport checked out. He was Henry Floyd, a citizen of the United Kingdom, and he was not required to have a visa to enter Australia. The photo looked recent enough and was a good match, and the passport was legitimate and cleared by the computer system.

The immigration official cracked a weak smile when he handed back the man's passport. "Enjoy your stay."

Henry Floyd nodded in brief acknowledgement, grabbed his cabin bag and headed for the customs area, where he knew he would be cleared for entry, as he carried nothing unlawful. He was spotlessly clean; a model international passenger.

Outside the airport building, the three men met at a previously-agreed position, and awaited the arrival of a van, which arrived two minutes ahead of schedule to pick them up. The black van's tyres squealed briefly when it came to a stop, and Henry Floyd opened the sliding passenger door.

Floyd glanced at his diver's watch. So far, things had gone smoothly and exactly according to plan. In less than half an hour, they would meet their client, Jock Speller.

24

Zelda woke up shivering. The air was not particularly cold, but she felt worn out and exposed, her body lacking the basic fuel to keep going. She had fallen asleep under a tree, exhausted from her experience the previous day, and then awoke with a start in the early morning hours. The sounds of the night; bird calls and scurrying noises, seemed to be all around her. The island clearly had an active night life.

She stood up shakily, too tired to even bother brushing the clinging sand from her body. Her skin was sticky from the sea air, her hair a nest of tangled ringlets sprinkled with sand. The moonlight shone through a break in the clouds, and she could see the restless motion of the waves in the distance.

Under different circumstances, the idea of waking on an island might have been a lot more pleasant, but Zelda felt alone and vulnerable. What if they were never found? For all she knew, the island was so isolated that it was completely ignored by passing ships. What if she was stuck on the island for months, years even? Zelda shook her head resolutely. That simply wouldn't happen, she told herself.

She licked her dry lips, and realised she had no fresh water to drink. What if there was no fresh water on the island at all?

She would have to think of her own survival, Zelda realised; find her own water, and something to eat.

Her arm ached, and Zelda lifted it up and held it closer to her face to inspect the plastic cast in the light from a dim and distant moon. The cast was still intact, though dirty and well-scuffed. The Glock pistol was still tucked into her shorts, and she touched it to reassure herself. Then she wrapped her arms around her body, and walked slowly through the half-darkness, avoiding obstacles and placing her feet very carefully.

Every now and again she heard a rustling sound from the bushes, and the occasional chirping of a cricket. She retraced her steps to the beach, and when she approached the ocean, began to feel slightly better. Maybe things weren't so bad after all, she reasoned, but the raging thirst burnt her throat and it made her slightly panicky regarding the need to find water.

She walked the length of the beach, reaching an outcrop of rocks. The sky was gradually growing lighter, and Zelda realised it was almost dawn. She looked up at the trees, able to discern their outlines and large branches. Then it occurred to her – palm trees, of course! Coconuts – and more importantly – coconut water!

With a renewed sense of energy, she began scanning the trees, trying to find coconut trees among them. Zelda walked faster and faster, excited by the prospect of finding the island's equivalent of pure gold. She stumbled slightly in the sand and passed one tree after the other – but failed to find a single coconut tree. Undaunted, she pressed on.

She finally came across a small cluster of trees; exactly what she'd been searching for. The trees were beautiful, standing tall and bearing fruit, but they stood on a slope, making them slightly more difficult to reach.

Zelda scrambled up the incline and when she reached the trees, she discovered they towered above her. Their height and smooth trunks made them almost impossible to climb. Her heart sunk. The coconuts were easy to spot, but seemingly impossible to reach.

She searched the foot of the nearest tree for fallen coconuts, but couldn't find any. Zelda pressed her lips together, to stop herself from bursting into tears. She wanted to scream her frustration to the skies.

But then she remembered the pistol tucked into her shorts. In desperation, she withdrew the Glock and held it in a trembling hand. Could she shoot a coconut from the tree?

Breathing deeply, she steadied her shooting hand, and lifted the pistol higher to take careful aim at the top of the coconut tree – her target a plump coconut near the centre of the cluster. She took aim at the stem and squeezed the trigger.

The coconut exploded with a sharp crack, showering coconut fragments and other debris over the ground. The coconut water rained down, and Zelda could feel the fine droplets landing on her face.

"Don't shoot!" She heard Jasper's voice, coming from somewhere near the bushy area next to the beach. "I'm coming out!" Moments later, he emerged from the bushes, awkwardly trying to fasten his pants, and simultaneously trying to raise a free hand.

"Don't shoot, for God's sake," he said again, staring at the pistol in Zelda's hand.

"I wasn't shooting at you," Zelda grumbled, annoyed at Jasper and more frustrated than ever about destroying the coconut. She lowered the pistol.

"You're just shooting randomly?" Jasper sounded puzzled.

He looked around, trying to work out what she had been aiming at.

Zelda evaded his question. "What were you doing – there in the bush?"

"My stomach… was a little upset," he said sheepishly.

"Dear Jesus." Zelda rolled her eyes.

"What?" Jasper said.

"It's that crap you've been eating," she said.

"What were you aiming at?" he asked again, ignoring her statement.

"I was trying to get a bloody coconut down from the tree, okay?"

Jasper sniggered, much to her annoyance.

"If you're trying to piss me off, you picked the wrong time," said Zelda. The cold threat hung heavily in the air.

Jasper lifted one hand, trying to reassure her. "If it's coconuts you want, I can get you coconuts," he said.

"You can?" Zelda asked. *Is this a trick?* she wondered.

Jasper pointed at the outcrop of rocks. "See those rocks? On the other side, just a little up the hill, you'll find plenty of them."

"If this is a joke…" she warned.

"I promise," he replied. "I'll show you if you want."

Zelda eyed him suspiciously for a moment, and then nodded in the direction of the rocks. "Lead the way."

"Would you mind putting that thing away?" he asked, watching the weapon still held firmly in her hand.

Zelda hesitated for a moment, then shoved the Glock into the front of her shorts. "Now can we go?"

Jasper led her to the rocks, and she followed behind at a safe distance, her stomach making a deep gurgling noise. "Can you walk faster?" she prodded.

Jasper obeyed.

It took them about fifteen minutes to clamber over the rocks, and make their way past numerous trees to another, smaller beach. On the far side, Zelda saw the palm trees. This cluster was more accessible. Some of the younger trees had not grown quite as tall, and as they approached, she saw several coconuts on the ground.

Ignoring her exhaustion, Zelda sprinted for the trees, leaving a surprised Jasper behind her. When she reached the nearest coconut, she sunk to her knees, scratching at its rough, stringy husk and looking around for a stick, a stone – anything – to break it open.

Jasper caught up with her, and seeing her desperate struggle, picked up another coconut and placed it on top of a rock that was barely visible above the sand line. He took a smaller, sharp rock and began stripping away the husk and then hitting the top of the coconut repeatedly in an attempt to crack the shell. Within a couple of minutes, he cracked the shell and then carefully removed the fragments.

He handed the coconut to Zelda, who grabbed it eagerly. She took large gulps of coconut water, spilling some of it on her T-shirt and emptied the entire coconut within a few seconds. The she paused, out of breath. "More," she said.

"Okay," said Jasper. "You should really—"

"More... please," she said.

Jasper nodded and set to work on another coconut.

25

Henry Floyd checked his watch before leading the other two men under his command into one of the Leadenhall Shipping warehouses at Marrickville. Jock Speller was waiting for them inside.

"Good morning, sir," Floyd said, suppressing the urge to salute.

The warehouse was under renovation, and the smell of paint hung in the air. The place was huge, and separated off into an administration wing, with a long corridor branching into a row of offices.

Jock Speller nodded a brief greeting, then led his three visitors into the administration wing, before directing them to one of the offices. The room was brightly lit by fluorescent tubes, and sparsely furnished; holding a few chairs and two long collapsible tables One table carried the 'equipment' – a small selection of automatic and semi-automatic weapons, knives, ammunition and personal communications devices. Floyd noticed hardware items such as plastic canisters, duct tape, and gloves were also piled on the table, along with a medical emergency kit.

"I tried to stick to your shopping list as closely as possible," Jock said dryly.

Floyd nodded, and approached the table to have a closer look. His two companions did the same.

They picked up some of the weapons to inspect them more closely, each man making a mental inventory. Floyd picked up the G-36 assault rifle and tested the weight in his hands. "I've been reliably told that its range is somewhat limited," said Jock, nodding at the weapon.

Floyd agreed. "It's designed for close quarters. That's all we need."

Jock's eyebrows rose slightly. "If you say so."

Floyd glanced at the other two men: "What do you say?"

They nodded, almost in unison, but Floyd caught a minor hesitation from one of them.

"Barry?" he said, waiting for a response.

"Grenades?" Barry questioned.

Floyd shook his head. "We may have to fly in with the client. And he's nervous about explosives. Same goes for heavy weapons."

Barry nodded. He obviously wasn't thrilled, but he knew better than to question Floyd's directions.

"Nathan?" Floyd waited for a response from the third man, but Nathan merely shook his head.

Floyd turned back to Jock Speller. "What do we know?" he asked.

"We're still tracking down the... targets," he said. "Once we do, we'll need to move out fast. I need you available, twenty-four hours a day."

"We do what it says in the contract," said Floyd.

Jock smiled grimly. "Good. Accommodation okay?"

"Just fine," said Floyd. He was not the type to chit-chat.

"Any concerns?"

"Just one," Floyd replied. "We don't usually take the client along for the ride. Too risky."

Jock had been waiting for this objection. "This project is... unusual," he said. "It's a personal matter. He wants to be there, in person."

"Highly irregular," said Floyd, still unhappy with the arrangement.

"We're not baby-sitters," Barry piped in.

"I think you'll find he's not your usual client. And we'll take full responsibility for his presence."

Floyd paused, thinking it over before he nodded slowly. "As long as you pick up the pieces," he said.

26

Silver Tambourine lived up to its reputation. The luxury motor yacht handled the open ocean well, and delivered enough power for Clive Edgewood and Bernard Kemp to make good time, especially cruising, as they were, at top speed.

Clive was at the helm, and he thought the skipper's cap, navy shirt and sunglasses he wore made him look like a character in a movie. He felt in control, and excitement bubbled in his chest. *Now this was an adventure!*

The enjoyment lasted until Bernard interrupted his thoughts. "So what's the plan?" the man asked, peering out to sea with a baseball cap drawn tightly over his head to keep the wind from blowing it off.

"The plan? The plan is to get our little lost sheep back – that's the plan," Clive said. He couldn't hide the annoyance in his voice..

"What if someone else gets to them first?"

Clive gave him a disappointed look. "Why don't you let me worry about the details? Trust me, I know my customers. I can read their minds."

"Brassington's not going to waste any time trying to get to us. You know that, right?"

"I have it under control. Brassington is a predictable animal. He'll try to throw money at cracking our security, but we've got so many layers of protection... Nick saw to that."

"I hope you're right," said Bernard, and kept staring grimly out to sea.

"You worry too much, pal," Clive said. "Why don't you help yourself to a beer? Relax. I'm going to need you fresh and rested when we arrive at our destination."

Bernard nodded, but he didn't move. He couldn't shake the feeling that things were not going to be as easy as Clive made them sound.

27

Jasper and Zelda had been sitting together and chewing on pieces of coconut for what seemed like hours. Once they had broken the pieces apart, their meal turned out to be rather tasty, and it served to keep their hunger at bay.

Their clothes were dirty, their hair stringy and their skin was covered by a fine layer of gritty sand. Jasper's shirt was torn after he'd caught it on a bush and blotches of dirt discoloured Zelda's shorts and T-shirt.

"Do you think we'll survive?" Zelda asked suddenly. "I mean, if they don't find us."

"Somebody will find us," Jasper replied. But his answer came across as hopeful, rather than confident.

"Are we going to live off coconuts?"

"We'll have to explore the place. See what else there is," Jasper said.

They were confined to one side of the island, because hills and rocky terrain made it difficult to reach the other wide.

"I think it's just us," said Zelda.

"People have been here," Jasper revealed.

Zelda paused, the piece of coconut she'd been eating stopping midway to her mouth. "What do you mean? How do you know?"

"I found a place. Some rubbish and stuff..."

Zelda rose to her feet. "Show me."

Jasper hesitated for a moment. "You're going to be disappointed," he said. "It's nothing much."

"Whatever," Zelda replied. "I still want to see it."

He led her towards the sandy patch between the trees, where he had found litter left by an unidentified group of visitors to the island. It was, of course, exactly the way he'd left it.

"See?" he said, pointing at an empty plastic bottle and a rusty food can.

Zelda was enthusiastic. "Could be useful," she announced. "Weren't you a boy scout?"

Jasper shook his head, and watched in surprise when Zelda sank down onto her hands and knees, scooping up handfuls of sand to see if anything else was buried in it.

"You never know..." she muttered.

Jasper scanned the surface of the sand to see if he could see anything useful among the rubbish before his attention returned to Zelda. There was something about her that captured his attention. Her breeze-curled hair looked beautiful, and her feisty attitude made her all the more alluring.

She looked up at him and lifted an eyebrow. "So? Aren't you going to help?"

"I... There's nothing here. This is just trash," he said.

But Zelda was undeterred. "Thanks a lot," she grumbled, and carried on with her search.

Jasper willed himself to look away – to avoid staring at her. His eye caught a tiny flash of colour, wedged between two branches in a nearby tree. It was glossy, and seemed to be a small piece of plastic. When he took a closer look, he noticed it had a cylindrical shape – and realised it was a disposable cigarette lighter. He was instantly excited, but discovered that the lighter was wedged in tight. It took quite a bit of wiggling to pull it free, but once it was in his hand Jasper was delighted. The metal cap at the top of the lighter was rusted, but at least it wasn't broken, and there appeared to be lighter fluid inside it.

"Look," he said, hardly believing his luck.

Zelda rose slowly to her feet and snatched the cigarette lighter out of his hand.

"Careful, don't—" he started to say.

"Wait," Zelda cut him short. She scanned the surface of the sand, then sunk back on to her knees and brushed aside the sand in a certain spot. Moments later, she produced what was left of a cigarette butt, put it in her mouth, and flicked the sparking mechanism on the lighter with shaky hands.

"What the hell..." said Jasper.

But Zelda ignored him, and tried repeatedly to get the lighter to work.

"You're kidding me," said Jasper. "That thing is gold and you want to light an old, used cigarette butt with it?"

Zelda's thumb repeatedly turned the tiny wheel at the top of the lighter – until the top of the lighter snapped off and fell in the sand.

"Shit," she said.

"Give it to me," Jasper said. He was angry, and took the lighter away from her, then searched the sand frantically until he found the top.

He stared at the two parts of the lighter, and looked as if he was about to cry. "You stuffed the whole thing up," he said.

"Well, of course," she replied. "Blame me for everything."

"Maybe we can…" Jasper began, searching his mind for ideas on getting the lighter to work.

"Can you fix it?"

Jasper stared at Zelda, incredulous. "What do you mean 'fix it'? How the hell am I going to fix it?"

Zelda merely shrugged.

Nearly half an hour later, Jasper kneeled in front of a flat rock. On top of the rock he had placed the remains of a rusted tin can, creating a shallow dish of sorts. Next to that he had assembled a few dry leaves and grasses, which would serve as kindling.

With a shaking hand, he poured a tiny quantity of the lighter fluid into his 'dish'. He pinched the top of the lighter tightly between two fingers and rolled his finger over the little rusted wheel. Almost at once he saw a tiny, fleeting spark, and he could barely contain his excitement. But when he tried again, and again, it failed to repeat itself.

Almost five minutes later, his fingers raw from the friction on the wheel, another spark appeared, and then another – and moments later, the lighter fluid ignited. Low blue flames sprang to life. Jasper trembled with excitement.

"Oh my god," said Zelda.

"Stay," Jasper said immediately. "Don't get close."

"Stay? What am I? A fucking dog?"

"Just…" Jasper began to say, but he noticed that the flame was burning very low. It was fast consuming the tiny bit of fuel.

He hastily, and yet as delicately as possible, put some of the grasses in the flame, then added one or two more. The flame suddenly switched to a yellowish colour as the grasses ignited. Larger flames flared up, and as he added further fuel, a small fire took hold.

"Shit, you did it!" shouted Zelda. She sounded utterly delighted.

28

The three men converged on what appeared to be a derelict building.

Using hand signals, Henry Floyd pointed Barry towards the rear of the building, to cover the back entrance. Nathan covered a side entrance, in case anyone tried to escape.

Carrying a Micro Uzi submachine gun at waist height, Floyd took up a position near the front entrance. He listened intently for the smallest sounds, but apart from a few bird noises the only other sound came from a construction site about two miles away.

The building was in the industrial quarter, close to the Botany Bay shipyards. The building had been used as an office during a land reclamation project years earlier. Now it served as a temporary storage place, used by the harbour authorities. From the looks of it, it hadn't been used for a long time. Some of the window panes were broken, and the building was badly in need of a coat of paint.

Still, the men remained cautious and tense, keeping out of sight as far as was possible.

Floyd peered in through the nearest window. It was dusty, but he could make out a bare room with a rudimentary concrete floor inside. The room seemed as if it hadn't been used for months, maybe even years. He advanced on to the next window, and repeated the process of searching for any signs of human activity. He found none.

At the back of the building, Barry was performing a similar task. Moving cautiously along the exterior wall of the building, he found an unlatched window, and inched it open slowly, avoiding noise. The gap allowed him to extend his arm inside and reach for the nearest door latch, which he managed to click open with the flip of his finger. He tested the door handle, and discovered the door was unlocked.

Icy calm, Barry fished his mobile phone out of his pocket and sent a noiseless text message to Floyd: "Back door open. Going in."

Floyd texted back a "Y" character, giving Barry the green light to proceed.

Barry moved silently into the large room at the back, stepping swiftly through to a smaller entrance hall in the front, a Glock-17 pistol held slightly ahead of him, ready to lift and fire at any moment. There was no sign of life and no detectable noises either.

Upon reaching the front door, he quietly unlatched it, allowing Floyd to enter. Leaving their third partner, Nathan, to guard the outside and alert them of unwanted visitors, the two men moved methodically from one room to the next, relying on hand signals to coordinate their movements.

Two of the rooms had wooden crates stored in them, and the men inspected the contents briefly before moving on. The rest of the building was empty, although they did find an electronic device attached to the wall near a power plug. It hadn't been plugged into the power socket, and closer investigation revealed it was powered by its own, small battery pack.

Floyd kneeled down next to the gadget. Taking out his phone, he tapped out a number on the touchscreen.

"Yes?" It was Jock Speller's voice which responded.

"Nobody home," said Floyd.

"Anything of interest?"

"A small gadget, mounted on the wall. It seems to be live – a transmitter, maybe," said Floyd. "You want me to bring it along?"

"No," came the reply. "It may trigger an alarm. I'll let the technical people have a look at it."

"Right," said Floyd. "We're coming home."

29

Silver Tambourine moored at Oyster Cove, on the island of Mellanima, that evening. Clive Edgewood had chosen the island as a refuelling stop, and they had made it to their destination slightly ahead of schedule.

Clive dealt with the paperwork at the customs office, while Bernard secured the vessel and stayed on board. The motor yacht did attract some attention in what was largely a fishing harbour, but Clive avoided conversation with the locals, to prevent giving out any information about their journey.

Clive treated himself to a dinner consisting of shellfish, prepared Cajun-style, along with some garlic bread and white wine. The café he selected overlooked the water, and its rough-hewn deck was supported by large timber posts, apparently structure left over from a jetty that had extended into the water years earlier.

It was pleasant enough, with simple kerosene lanterns casting a warm glow over the tables. The evening was warm, with a light breeze blowing, and Clive enjoyed being able to relax on land.

His dinner arrived on a large tray, carried by handsome,

young, dark-haired man who appeared to have Pacific Islander blood running through his veins. He had a willing, friendly smile and his teeth shone white in the glow of the lanterns.

"Beautiful evening," said Clive, and smiled at him.

"Beautiful," the young man repeated, and grinned widely.

Clive guessed that he wasn't a native English speaker. *French perhaps,* he thought, remembering that the island had been a French colony in the distant past. Some of the locals preferred a pidgin French that few outsiders could decipher. "Clive," he said. "My name is Clive."

"My name Michel," said the young man.

"Are you the owner? Of this café?"

Michel's grin widened. "No, no. My... um, father," he explained. "You... make tourist?"

Clive smiled at his expression, and wanted to shake his head, but then decided to go with it. "Yes, tourist," said Clive. "With a boat." He pointed towards the boats moored in the harbour.

"Ah," Michel said. "You a rich man."

Clive smiled at him and nodded. "Yes. I'm rich," he agreed confidently. "Maybe you can tell me, Michel – where can I... have a bit of fun on this island?"

"Fun, monsieur?" Michel said, repeating the word carefully. "You want music? Dancing?"

Clive gestured with a crooked finger for Michel to come closer, and when the younger man leaned in, Clive touched his forearm. "I'm looking for a girl... or a boy," he said in a quiet voice.

"Ah," Michel said, and his expression confirmed that he understood. "You want... the fun." He smiled broadly again.

"When do you finish here? When do you finish work?"

"Me, monsieur?" Michel clearly hadn't expected Clive's request to be directed at him. "Later, monsieur. Later. Um.... why you...?" He was searching for the words.

"Why don't you show me around?" Clive suggested. "Show me where the fun is?"

Michel looked surprised, but not unwilling. "Well, monsieur, I..." Then his face lit up with another winning smile. "Yes... I can," he said.

30

Jasper had built a large fire from driftwood, using handfuls of twigs and dry leaves for kindling. He and Zelda sat side by side, without saying much, just enjoying the warmth. A flattened stainless steel can they'd found was positioned on the hot coals near the fire. On it were the remaining bits of mussels and strips of seaweed that Jasper had cooked.

"It's weird, but it feels a bit like a holiday," Zelda said. "Reminds me of a back-packing trip in Greece."

"It's great," Jasper agreed. "I never expected..." He stopped talking and stared at Zelda. She looked beautiful in the light from the flickering fire. *Her lips...*

"I'm sorry," she said, "that I fucked up the lighter."

He smiled at her. "Hey, we got a fire going. We're doing alright."

She nodded.

"Of course it would be nice if we had a bed," he said, quickly adding, "to sleep in." Just in case she took offence at his suggestion.

Zelda had a faint smile on her face, as she stared into the fire. "What will you do... if and when we get back?" she asked.

Jasper shrugged. "I don't know if I'll still have a job," he said. "I suppose we'll have to tell the cops," he suggested hesitantly.

Zelda turned to him. "Maybe it's not so bad," she said, "disappearing for a while."

"What will you do?"

"Go back to my old life, I suppose."

"What did you do... before? Of course, you don't have to tell me anything if—"

"My dad's rich," she said flatly. "I did whatever the fuck I wanted."

"Right," he replied, deciding not to probe any further.

"He's an arsehole," she added quietly.

"Who?"

"My dad. He's a fucking arsehole."

"We all feel that way about—"

Zelda cut him short. "No, you don't know him. Always gets what he wants. It's always his way."

"You could just leave," said Jasper.

"Tried that," she replied.

"I'm sorry."

"Tell me something nice," she said a minute later. "Who's waiting for you? Do you have kids? What makes you happy?"

"No kids, no wife," he admitted. "I've got a couple of buddies. We drink, watch rugby... it's nothing much."

"Fuck, that's boring," she said. "And I thought *my* life was in the toilet."

"Thanks."

"Sorry, I'm just pissed at my own life; that's what it is."

"That's okay. You don't hold back much, do you?"

She shrugged.

Maybe you should take a holiday... after this," Jasper said.

"Tried that, many times," she said. "Skiing in Switzerland, playing fucking bongo drums in Jamaica. I couldn't settle down."

"What's the—?" he began, but he was interrupted again before he could finish his thought.

"If I don't find a fag soon, I think I'm going to fucking lose it," Zelda announced.

Jasper stared at her. "You're still thinking about smoking?"

"What else is there?" she said, shrinking back into her sandy hollow and crossing her arms.

Their conversation dried up, each of them staring into the fire and occasionally glancing around when noises broke the silence around them.

Zelda stood up and shook some sand off her shorts, then rubbed at her arms. "I still feel cold," she said. "My arms..." She indicated the spot where Jasper was sitting. "Do you mind?"

"Of course," said Jasper, surprised that she would want to sit with him, even if it was only for warmth.

Zelda nestled in beside him, and Jasper wrapped his arm around her. "Pity we forgot to bring a blanket," he joked, smiling. "Sorry, not funny," he added.

Zelda didn't reply, merely wriggling into a more comfortable position. Then she sighed heavily.

Jasper held her closely, sharing as much of his body warmth as possible.

"That's nice," he heard her murmur. She lowered her head to his chest.

31

Norman Brassington's hotel room reeked of alcohol, and his breath carried a heavy smell of whisky. Jock Speller sat next to him on the large sofa. It was past midnight.

"They... erm, sent it through," said Norman, his voice slurred. He pointed at the coffee table, where a printed email message was wedged in next to a large fruit bowl.

Jock had already seen it, because Leroy and his team had intercepted the message. "I know," he said gently. "It's a Swiss bank account. They want the money deposited within two days."

Norman didn't reply. He continued to stare blankly at the opposite wall.

"Have you had some sleep?" Jock asked.

Brassington shook his head.

"We're not far off. We can track them down," said Jock.

Brassington grunted, and waved his hand limply, as if dismissing the idea that they would ever locate the kidnappers.

"It will be better if you can get some rest. We'll have to move fast when we track them down."

"You believe them?" said Brassington slowly. "You trust... them?"

Jock nodded. "They'll get the job done."

Brassington nodded. "Jock, I..." His voice trailed off.

"We'll get them, Norm," said Jock. He squeezed Brassington's arm, trying to reassure him.

32

When Clive Edgewood reached the *Silver Tambourine*, he met with a hostile Bernard.

"Where the fuck were you?"

Clive pasted on his usual, easy smile. "Business, pal. You know how it goes."

"Could have told me you were going to make a night of it," Bernard complained.

"Arrangements to take care of – you know that. I found a computer I could use, with an internet connection."

"You used an unsecured machine?" Bernard was immediately angry about the security risk.

"Relax, will you?" Clive took a USB drive out of his pocket. "I used this. Nick fixed it up for me. Connects securely on any machine."

Bernard didn't reply, and remained unconvinced.

"Why don't you relax? Get some sleep," Clive suggested. "Tomorrow's going to be a long day, and we're starting early."

Bernard nodded slowly. "Just want you to know. You compromise this, and I'm out. Consider this a friendly warning."

He turned, and Clive saw a pistol tucked into the back of his pants.

"You worry too much, pal," Clive muttered as Bernard descended the steps to below decks. Although Bernard's behaviour did leave a tingle of worry in the back of his mind.

33

Jasper lay on his back, completely naked, with Zelda in a sitting position on top of him; riding him. She groaned loudly, and her fingernails cut into the skin on his chest. As their rhythm increased, he watched her breasts dance wildly over his face, tempting him. She arched her back and moaned, before suddenly throwing herself forward again.

She convulsed, a shiver rippling through her body before she settled quietly on his chest, breathing heavily.

"Fuck," she whispered.

Jasper wrapped his arms around her and held her tight, her warmth enveloping him.

She shuddered again, then lay still. Her hips moved almost imperceptibly, her sweaty skin brushing against his own. He detected a wild animal-like smell on her body – in her hair, in her perspiration. He kissed her bare shoulder, and tasted the saltiness.

She turned to face him. "Hey," she said, smiling.

He kissed her, lingering at her mouth for a little while and taking pleasure in their lips touching, and the sensation of his tongue against hers. They breathed in unison, as if locked into a strangely synchronised rhythm, both sucking in long deep breaths of ocean air.

Jasper ran his hands slowly down her sides. He lingered at her buttocks, and then slipped his hands down to her thighs.

"Hey, are you feeling me up, mister?" she questioned, grinning.

"Damn right," he said, and grinned back at her.

She kissed him lightly, then rolled away, finding a comfortable position in the sand alongside him, their naked bodies glittering sensuously in the flickering light of the fire.

They were both completely relaxed and yet aware, hyper-aware, of the sounds of the night; the rustle of the breeze in the trees, the sound of waves breaking on the rocks.

Jasper watched the fire. It was already beginning to burn low, and he would have to find more wood to keep it going throughout the night. Now and again, the wood popped and sent a tiny spark flying heavenwards, joining the millions of bright stars visible in the night sky above them.

"What are you thinking?" Zelda asked.

"My mind is completely blank," he replied. "You turned it into mush."

She chuckled.

Both of them drifted off into languid sleep.

Nearly an hour later, Jasper woke up with a start and sat upright. Zelda was no longer by his side. *Where had she gone?*

He scrambled to his feet, alarmed that the fire had burnt down so low, only a few flames flickering between the remaining glowing coals.

"Zelda?" he called. It was the first time he'd spoken her name, and it felt unfamiliar on his tongue. "Zelda?" he repeated more loudly.

There was no reply.

The pre-dawn light was beginning to appear on the horizon. Jasper noticed that Zelda's clothes were still in the small, untidy pile she'd left them in, but the Glock was missing.

He stumbled across the dimly lit terrain, and stubbed his toe against a rock. "Aghh! Bugger!" he complained, and limped on. Maybe she had simply needed to use a bush toilet, he reasoned. But why had she taken the pistol with her? Did she still not trust him?

He found the same natural pathway between the trees that he'd used the day before. It led further up the hill, from where he would have a better vantage point. He scrambled up the hill, keeping a look-out for any movement.

A few birds fluttered out of a nearby tree, but there was no other movement. Jasper was beginning to feel slightly foolish, walking by himself, stark naked. He was about to turn back when he heard a noise. It sounded like a shout – a human voice – in the distance. Could it be that Clive had already located the island? Jasper began running in the direction of the sound.

When he reached the top of the hill, he was struggling for air. He paused to catch his breath, and caught a movement from the corner of his eye. It was Zelda, winding her way downhill towards the small cove below them. Then he saw what she was heading towards – a motorised dinghy, with four men standing nearby. They seemed to be unaware of her approach.

"Zelda," he hissed loudly. "Zelda! Stop!"

But she either couldn't hear him, or she didn't care.

"Hello!" He heard her call out to the men. "We're up here! Can you help us?"

"Zelda! No!" he shouted, not bothering to keep his voice low.

She stopped in her tracks, and stared up at him in disbelief. "What? We can go with them, get off this island!" she shouted back.

Jasper shook his head in warning. "They're smugglers! They'll kill you!" He glanced nervously at the beach. The men had heard them and were taking an interest. One man had a rifle slung over his shoulder and as Jasper watched, he slipped the strap off his shoulder and lifted the weapon defensively.

"What?" she said. "How do you know?"

"I found ammunition... on the beach!" he said, his voice slightly quieter. "Don't trust them, for God's sake."

"Are you fucking with me?" she shrieked.

A shot rang out, the bullet whistling through the air and hitting a nearby tree. Jasper ducked instinctively, then checked to see what Zelda was doing.

"Holy fuck, they're shooting at us!" Zelda shouted. She remained frozen in place for just a moment, before she began running further up the hill.

"Come over here!" Jasper yelled, as a second shot rang out.

He heard an excited voice shouting from the beach and imagined it was one of the men giving orders. The men stopped shooting and started running up the hill. Two of the men wore headbands, making them clearly visible against the green foliage.

"Run!" Jasper shouted. It was unnecessary, because Zelda was already sprinting. A few moments later, she was by his side, and they ran into the denser bush together. They crashed through branches and swept smaller bushes aside as they ran.

"Why the fuck didn't you tell me?" Zelda managed to growl.

"Didn't want you to panic," Jasper tried to shout, but he could hardly get the words out. It felt as if sheer panic had closed his throat, shutting down his vocal cords.

They stopped for a moment, hidden from view, trying to catch their breath.

"What now?" Zelda demanded.

"We need to disappear," Jasper said. His skin felt clammy and he suspected he was going to throw up. "We've got to hide."

"Maybe we can talk to them..." Zelda suggested.

"Are you kidding? They'll shoot us. They'll rape you and fucking sell you to the highest bidder afterwards. Do you understand?"

Zelda stood in stunned silence for a moment. "Well?" she demanded. "What are we going to do?"

"Come on," said Jasper. He began running again, leading the way further uphill towards the dense vegetation on the other side of the island.

34

Nick Bennett thought he'd heard something, and peeked out of the window. He had been holed up in the apartment for days, and his nervousness had increased as each hour passed.

He was so fearful, he'd even refused to take out the garbage, despite Clive's insistence that he should carry on life as usual, to avoid raising suspicions among the neighbours.

Now he was in the grip of severe cabin fever. Every noise, every car arriving outside jangled his nerves. He'd started smoking again, as he knew he would, and was living off soup, stale bread, canned food and frozen pizza. He'd started suffering headaches from a lack of sleep, and regularly caught himself staring at his computer screens for an hour or more at a time, without doing anything constructive.

He had checked the Swiss account online for the umpteenth time, battling the bank's elaborate security measures before being allowed to log in. Not surprisingly, no payment had been made. The deadline hadn't been reached yet, so there was nothing to do but wait.

Nick stood up, stretched, and surveyed the room, seeing nothing but litter; empty cans, discarded newspapers, dirty plates and empty packets. He could smell his own body odour and realised it was high time he took a shower. It was just so difficult to leave his computer for longer than a few minutes. *So difficult.*

He sighed, snatching up a plastic bag and throwing some of the rubbish into it, before he chucked the bag into a corner. He tore off his T-shirt and sniffed it gingerly, discovering the sweaty odour emanating from the material was overwhelming. Disgusted, he threw the T-shirt on top of the discarded rubbish bag and went for a shower.

With the hot water pelting onto his skin, he almost felt alive again. It was like an emotional release after the strain of the past few days, and he forced his problems to the back of his mind, even if it was only for a few minutes.

Stepping out of the shower, Nick rubbed his scalp vigorously with a towel and then ran his fingers through his tangled hair. Some of the hair came off in his hands. He stared in dismay at the loose black hairs for a few moments. "God," he said to the bathroom mirror. "I'm totally going bald."

He heard a tiny noise from outside the bathroom door and the stomach-clenching fear immediately returned. He wrapped a towel around his waist before stepping out of the bathroom to have a good look around.

The balcony window was open, and a breeze lifted the curtain slightly. It was a low-rise building of only two levels, and Nick was certain he'd closed the window securely. Could he have been so careless? *What's the use of being neurotic, if you leave the window open?*

Stepping across some discarded rubbish on the carpet, he strode over to the window, closed it and secured the latch. Then he plotted a path across the carpet to the bedroom, where he had the computers set up. But when he entered the room, he discovered a man – a muscular man – seated in his chair, watching his computer screens!

"What the fuck?" Nick shouted.

Even as he yelled, Nick heard a noise behind him and instinctively swung around, but it was already too late. Something hit his head, just above the ear. The blow was hard enough for his vision to blur and then explode into a kaleidoscope of colours as he sank to his knees.

With panic rising in his chest, Nick tried to crawl on all fours across the carpet, barely holding on to consciousness as nausea rose swiftly in his stomach. He moved clumsily, desperate to get further away from his attacker.

His assailant put a short rubber truncheon back into his coat pocket, and smiled coldly at Nick's pathetic efforts to escape.

"He's pretty useless, Floyd" he told the other man, who was sitting in the chair in front of Nick's computer screens. "Won't put up much of a fight."

"Ah well," Floyd replied. "This shouldn't take long then."

Nick was only vaguely aware that they were discussing him. "What...?" he questioned, trying desperately to get his mind to focus.

The one named Floyd stood up, stopping Nick's forward movement by putting his boot on Nick's fingers and pressing down hard. Nick cried out in pain.

Floyd released Nick's fingers and kneeled down beside him on one knee. He lifted Nick's face between his thumb and forefinger, squeezing his cheeks. "Barry and I are going to ask you a few questions. Now I trust you're going to be a good boy," he said. "It'll be so much better for you."

Nick stared up into Floyd's eyes, and fear gripped his heart. He could see no mercy there, no empathy. He imagined this man could take him apart piece by piece if he wanted to – and wouldn't give a damn if he did.

Floyd and Barry grabbed Nick's arms, lifting him up until he stood unsteadily on his feet. Nick found it difficult to keep his balance, and his sight was still slightly blurry, making him fear he had a concussion. Floyd continued to grip his arm, while Barry brought two dining chairs into the room, and they forced Nick to sit down on one. They taped his wrists and forearms to the armrests, and his ankles to the wooden legs.

The two men worked quickly, efficiently. Floyd positioned the second chair in front of Nick, watching his eyes closely for the slightest reaction.

"Just a few tips," Floyd announced. "If you try to alert the neighbours by screaming, I will stuff socks into your mouth to keep you quiet, and then break your bones one by one. Understood?"

Nick's forehead glistened with sweat. He was still bewildered by the events of the past few minutes, and imagined he resembled a cornered animal to these two men.

"Do you understand?" Floyd snapped.

Nick nodded rapidly.

"Now I want you to tell me everything you have going on here," said Floyd. "The little system you have set up, the plan, the bank details, everything."

"Please," Nick whispered. "This wasn't my plan. I just set up the computers, that's all. I swear."

"Tell me your name."

Nick remained silent for a moment, thinking furiously, before he responded cautiously. "Nick."

"Rightio, Nick, I want all the details. Let's start with your full name," Floyd said.

"My full name is Nick... Longford," he said.

Floyd stared at him intently for a few moments, making Nick squirm uncomfortably. "You know what, Nick? I don't think you're being entirely straight with us. If you won't even tell me your real name, we're off to a very poor start."

"God, please, you've got to listen to me," Nick pleaded. "I didn't..."

Floyd picked up one of Nick's dirty socks from the carpet, rolled it into a tight ball, and began to shove it into Nick's mouth. Nick protested violently, and tried to bite down on Floyd's fingers, but Floyd slapped him hard with the flat of his hand. The slap made Nick's ears ring. He shook his head and tears rolled down his cheeks.

"Open your mouth," Floyd demanded, and when Nick didn't respond, he slapped him a second time. Nick's head jerked to one side and a fleck of blood appeared on his lip where the skin had split.

Floyd gripped Nick's head firmly and thrust the rolled-up sock into his mouth; this time with little resistance. Floyd picked up a roll of masking tape and tore off a length, sticking it over Nick's mouth, to prevent him from spitting out the sock.

Nick watched with wide eyes as Barry unzipped a backpack he'd been carrying, and took out a small, short-handled club hammer. He kneeled down by Nick's bare feet, lifted the hammer high, and struck one foot, instantly crushing two of Nick's toes. Nick tried to scream, but the sound was muffled by the sock and masking tape covering his mouth. When the shock of the blow had subsided slightly, Nick sobbed. Snot ran out of his nose and he struggled to breathe. Urine pooled on the seat beneath him and trickled down the leg of the chair.

Floyd leaned in closer to Nick. "We'll start with your feet, then we're going to break your hands, your legs, and keep going until you tell us everything we want to know. If you pass out, we'll revive you and start again. Do you understand?"

Nick lowered his head and sobbed brokenly. He was already a beaten man.

"Do you understand?" Floyd yelled, and when Nick didn't respond, he nodded at Barry, who lifted the hammer a second time, crushing another toe.

Nick screamed loudly through the sock, and tugged hard at his restraints before he slumped forward, crying and muttering unintelligibly.

"Do you understand?" Floyd asked again.

Nick nodded frantically and a trickle of blood flowed from his snotty nose.

"Right. I'm going to take the sock out of your mouth," Floyd said. "If you scream and shout, we'll start from the beginning again. Do you understand?"

Nick nodded desperately, quite certain he was going to die.

35

Jasper's body was covered with red scratches from the bushes they'd rushed past, trying to keep ahead of their pursuers. Zelda followed behind him, struggling to keep up. Her breath was hoarse in her throat, and she sounded as if she was about to collapse.

They ascended to the top of the first hill, then ran down the other side, tripping and falling here and there, sometimes skidding on the steeper slopes. Then up the next hill, and along an escarpment until they reached an area of denser vegetation – a better place to hide, Jasper thought.

"I can't go on!" Zelda gasped. He stopped and turned around, to discover Zelda was doubled over and heaving as if she was about to throw up. Instead, she spat on the ground, and then gave Jasper a pleading look.

"Just a little further," Jasper urged. "In the bushes, there." He pointed to a spot that promised thick green cover – an ideal place to hide. He grabbed Zelda's arm and tugged her forward, onwards. "Come on, stay with me," he said.

"Our tracks," she said, looking back at the tracks they'd left in the sandy soil. "They can follow us."

"We'll think of something," he said. "Come on!"

They ventured further into the thicker bush, pausing here and there to select paths leading slightly further up the hill, hoping to get a better vantage point. The soil was firmer here and they were leaving fewer tell-tale footprints. In the distance, they heard voices, shouting. The sound carried well in the sea air, and it sounded as if the men were already drawing closer.

Jasper spotted a tree on which some of the branches had been flattened, possibly by a storm. The low-hanging branches had continued to grow, providing a thick canopy close to the ground. "There!" he said, and pulled Zelda along by the arm.

They crouched down underneath the branches and found that they provided a roomy, sheltered area, invisible to anyone from the other side.

"Here," Jasper said. "Let's wait here." He searched the sand, hoping to find anything they could use as a weapon.

Zelda collapsed onto the leaf-strewn ground, breathing heavily, and moaning from the exertion. "Mother of God," she groaned. "I have never...."

Jasper shushed her. "They're getting close. We must be very quiet."

Zelda took his advice and they both listened intently. The voices were uncomfortably close. *What if they were found?*

Straining his ears for sounds coming from outside their hideout, Jasper noticed that Zelda no longer carried the Glock. "Where's the gun?" he whispered. "Didn't you have it with you?"

"I dropped it," she hissed, sounding exhausted.

"Dropped it?" Jasper was devastated. That weapon might have been their only hope.

"I fell... and bumped myself on— I lost it okay?" she whispered hoarsely.

"Okay, okay," he whispered.

The voices of the men were drawing much closer now.

Jasper discovered a flat stone, half-buried in the sand, and gripped it in his fist. He wasn't going down without a fight, he decided grimly.

36

Bernard was at the helm of the *Silver Tambourine* while Clive Edgewood studied the maps and checked the compass. It was a beautiful day, and the ocean was relatively calm, so they were making good time.

"Ahoy!" Bernard shouted, pointing at something in the distance.

Clive frowned, rising from his seat on the aft deck.

"Something's floating on the water!" Bernard shouted above the noise of the engines. He lifted the binoculars to his eyes and focused on the reflective object in the water, his other hand absent-mindedly caressing the steering wheel's teak trim.

Clive joined him at the helm. "What do you see?" he asked.

"Dunno," Bernard said, squinting. "It's difficult to make out."

"Let's take a closer look." Clive unhooked the binoculars from around Bernard's neck and lifted them to his own eyes. With the benefit of the extra magnification, he could see the object more clearly. It had a white, reflective upper surface and rose and dropped with the motion of the waves. Unfortunately, it was impossible to identify from such a distance.

"Could be part of a plane," said Clive. "We've passed the spot where we lost contact, but it could have drifted here from the crash site."

Approaching the object, Bernard reduced their speed and they coasted slowly closer. Once they were drifting alongside the object, both Bernard and Clive peered over the side. It certainly looked as if the object belonged to a plane.

"It looks like one of the floats," Clive said. "Maybe the plane broke up."

"Maybe they're gone," Bernard suggested thoughtfully.

Clive shook his head. "My guess is they're still alive. I checked out the pilot. Boring as hell. He stuck with all the safety rules – never had an incident in years. They would have had life jackets, at least."

"What could have taken them down?" said Bernard.

"I'm guessing Monty's caused all this shit," said Clive. "Son of a bitch."

"How do you know?"

Clive didn't reply immediately. "He's had problems," he finally said.

"What sort of problems?"

"Emotional problems, post-traumatic stress, whatever the hell they call it now," said Clive.

"And you let him fly along?" Bernard stared at Clive accusingly.

"Hey, he's the best man for the job, even if he is a little... unstable," Clive protested.

Bernard shook his head. "Wacked out of his fucking mind, you mean."

Clive ignored him. "There are plenty of islands 'round here. My guess is they made land somewhere."

"That's one pretty big guess," Bernard muttered.

"Lighten up," said Clive. "Let's take a look at the maps. If we go with the current, we'll know which way they most likely went, right?"

Bernard watched him sceptically and didn't reply.

37

Norman Brassington was a tough man, but even he was taken aback by the scene that he discovered inside the apartment.

Nick was still taped to the chair, his head hanging low and matted hair partially covering his bloody face. One of his feet and his left hand had been transformed into a pulpy mess. The room reeked of sweat and urine and there were numerous blood stains on the carpet.

"Is he dead?" Brassington asked hoarsely.

Floyd shook his head. "Just unavailable currently."

Jock Speller, who had followed Brassington into the apartment, turned his attention to the other two men. If he experienced any measure of shock or surprise, he didn't reveal it. "Do you have the information?" he asked.

Floyd nodded. He picked up a notebook, opening it to the most recent page. "Interrogation started at—" he began.

Brassington cut him short. "Where are they keeping her?" he demanded. The question had been eating away at his brain like acid for days now.

Floyd hesitated, glancing at Jock Speller first, before replying to Brassington. "He told us... they took her by aircraft, and they lost track of it along the way."

"What do you mean?" Brassington asked. "Lost track?"

"They had a transmitter on board," Floyd explained, "but they lost the transmitter signal somewhere along the way. It went dead. Only thing they have is the last-known location."

Brassington was stunned. He was silent, processing the new information and the implications it might have for his daughter's life.

"At first, I thought he was lying to us, but now I think he was telling the truth after all," Floyd said, glancing down at Nick's broken and bleeding body.

"What does that mean?" Brassington asked, his voice very quiet now. "What does that mean... exactly?"

"Did the plane go down?" Jock Speller demanded. "Do you know if it definitely did?" He sounded anxious, as if it had been his own daughter on the missing plane.

"There's no way of telling," replied Floyd. "But your abductor is on his way there now – by boat."

38

Zelda gripped Jasper's arm, leaving pink, finger-sized pressure marks. Jasper was aware of her naked body rubbing up against him, but right at the moment, he was too afraid to enjoy the sensation.

They waited, and listened, lying quietly beneath the leafy cover. They heard a sound here and there, but their pursuers remained quiet most of the time, only calling out at one another every now and again.

One of them came in closer. Jasper could hear his footsteps when he was on the soil, but the sound vanished when he reached a sandy patch.

Jasper held his breath, and he could tell Zelda was doing the same. She nearly screamed when a small bird fluttered by unexpectedly and her fingers squeezed Jasper's arm even harder.

Agonising minutes later, it sounded as if the men had moved further away. They heard a voice from further down the hill, and another behind them. It seemed as if at least one of the men had passed by their hiding place and was making his way up the next hill.

Then they heard the crackling of a two-way radio. A voice hissed and crackled, and it was clear the reception was poor. One of the men replied to the radio message, his voice growing louder.

Jasper and Zelda couldn't understand what the man was saying, although some English slang was interspersed throughout the conversation. The voice coming over the radio sounded tense, fretful. Moments later, the man who had responded to the radio message called out. It sounded like he was giving orders to the other two men again.

There was some excited jabbering, and from what Jasper could make out, it sounded as if the men were embroiled in a heated discussion.

Jasper shifted slightly on the sand, trying to relieve a cramp in his leg. Zelda looked at him in alarm.

"What the fuck are you doing?" she whispered.

"Nothing," he whispered back. "Just..." he groaned, not completing the sentence.

The discussion among their pursuers had died down, and it sounded as though they were moving away. *Maybe heading back?* Jasper lifted his head slightly, trying to peer through the leaves in the direction the men voices carried from.

"If they see you... I swear to God," Zelda hissed furiously. Jasper sunk back down to his previous position, and lay still, waiting.

The voices trailed off into the distance, making Jasper believe they were heading back to where they'd come from. Suddenly, a shot rang out – fired from a distance. Then they heard another shot.

"What the hell's happening?" Zelda demanded, but Jasper

shushed her. "They're leaving. I want to see what's going on!" Zelda protested.

"Are you crazy?"

"They're leaving. Maybe somebody's been shot at the beach," she said.

"You're staying right here," Jasper commanded.

"Fuck you," Zelda said, and stood up.

"They'll see you! You'll get shot."

As if in response to his words, they heard more shots, fired in quick succession. And then nothing, just an eerie silence which only succeeded in making Jasper more nervous.

Zelda shook her head stubbornly and crawled away from him. For an instant, Jasper thought about grabbing her, but immediately realised what a bad strategy that would be. "Zelda!" he said in a loud whisper, but she moved on, leaving their hiding place.

After a few moments of indecision, Jasper followed her. But when he crawled out from under the bushy branch, Zelda was already out of sight. *Now where?*

Zelda tip-toed until she was certain the men were gone, and then ran down a narrow sandy strip that led in the direction of the beach. The men were nowhere to be seen. She assumed they were somewhere ahead of her, but she stopped dead when she heard a man's voice from nearby. *"Berhenti"*. The word wasn't recognizable, but his tone of voice was loud, threatening.

The dark-skinned man carried a semi-automatic rifle. He wore a tattered pair of cargo shorts, and his vest was a dirty grey. He had what seemed to be a hand-crafted shell necklace around his neck, and his eyes grew wide when he realized that Zelda was completely naked.

He was young – barely twenty, Zelda guessed.

"*Datang,*" he said, waving her closer. When she didn't respond, he sounded angrier. "*Datang!*"

Just as he yelled at her, Zelda saw Jasper appear behind him, quietly moving closer.

Zelda had to distract the man, if Jasper was going to have any hope of reaching him without being shot. "Hmm?" she said blankly. She tried to think of something to say – anything.

The young man's eyes scanned her body, lingering on her breasts. Zelda seized the opportunity, lifting her hands slowly and cupping her breasts, wiggling slightly from side to side.

"Is this what you want to see?" she questioned. But his eyes had moved from her breasts to her groin. She lowered her hand there, playing with her pubic hair lightly with her fingers.

"Come on," she coaxed, her eyes never leaving the young man's face.

Jasper had finally gotten close enough. He held the flat stone he'd found in the hideaway in his hand, and moved forward swiftly, hitting the young man hard on the side of the head. The man sunk to his knees, blood gushing from the wound on his head. But even as he went down, he tried to turn around to face his attacker, rifle still in his hands.

Jasper stepped forward and hit him again, high on the cheekbone, near his eye. He collapsed backwards, and the rifle fell to the ground.

Uncannily, he raised his head again, and Jasper hit him again, and again, until he lay still.

Jasper stared at the bloody stone in his hand and dropped it, shocked by his own actions.

"Get the gun!" Zelda shrieked.

"Shit, he's finished…" Jasper muttered, surprised that he was capable of inflicting so much injury. He stared in horror at the young man's bleeding face.

"Get the gun, for fuck's sake!" Zelda repeated.

Jasper felt as if he was in a dream, no, a nightmare. He picked up the rifle and tested the weight in his hands. It felt heavy, unfamiliar. It occurred to Jasper that he was holding a murder weapon.

"Now we have a chance," Zelda said triumphantly.

39

Bernard spotted the island first, and pointed Clive towards it. "What a beauty," said Clive, smiling widely. "I had a feeling about this."

They headed straight for the island, until they spotted another boat in the vicinity. It appeared to be a fishing vessel at first, but something about it didn't look right. There was nobody on the deck and no markings on the vessel. The boat looked tired, neglected, even from this distance.

"See it?" Bernard questioned. "Looks abandoned."

Clive scanned the boat with the binoculars. "There's someone on board," he said. "I saw movement."

"Probably locals. Fishermen maybe?" Bernard said. He slowed the *Silver Tambourine* slightly. They were going to cut across the other boat's bow, and something about the other vessel was making Bernard uneasy. "Why don't you take the wheel?" he suggested to Clive. "Let me take a look at it, just to be on the safe side..."

Moments later, a man appeared on the deck of the other boat and fired two shots at the *Silver Tambourine*. One missed, whistling through the air, while the other hit the hull with a loud smack.

"Christ!" Clive shouted. He glanced up at the helm, only to discover that Bernard had already abandoned it, and was rapidly making his way below deck, where he'd stored his sniper rifle.

The motor yacht had slowed to a crawl, the engines idling. Clive crouched behind one of the bulkheads, popping his head out now and again to try and catch sight of the person on the other boat. The shooting had stopped. *Maybe they'd been warning shots to keep them away,* he thought.

Moments later, Bernard reappeared, carrying the RSASS sniper rifle. He was judging the distance as he moved and making an adjustment to the scope. Clive could see that Bernard had turned hunter. His movements were controlled, and cat-like. He moved quietly back up to the open deck, and crouched down, peering over the gunwale at the other boat.

Clive shrunk back into his hiding place behind the bulkhead, and waited. This was Bernard's territory.

Bernard took a few deep breaths, deliberately slowing his breathing before lifting the rifle and positioning it so that he had the other boat in his sights. At first, there was no movement visible, but then he saw it – a shadow moving past the window in the steering cabin. For a brief moment, the man was clearly outlined in the rifle scope. Without hesitation, Bernard fired a few shots in rapid succession and saw the man fall.

"Did you get him?" Clive asked from his hiding place.

Bernard nodded. "One down," he said.

"Are there... others?"

"Take us closer," Bernard said, his gaze still locked on to the other boat. When he noticed that Clive wasn't moving, he added, "Now."

Clive obeyed, moving cautiously to the helm station and taking control of the motor yacht.

As they approached the other boat, Bernard positioned himself near the bow, fully alert and looking out for any movement.

There was nothing to be seen. The other boat gave the appearance of being a ghost vessel. Bernard could hear it creaking as it moved about on the waves. Its hull was rusted, and the timberwork bleached from overexposure to the sun. If it was once a fishing vessel, it had long stopped functioning as one.

"Take us alongside," he instructed Clive.

Clive manoeuvred the motor yacht slowly closer and alongside the other vessel, while Bernard made his way to the aft deck, from where he would have better access to jump across. He held his rifle at the ready, scanning the deck for movement, but saw none.

The other boat was similar in length to the motor yacht, and in the calm waters and with the two boats at an even keel, Bernard was able to jump across. He landed on the other boat's deck with a thud, and waited a moment or two for a response, but received nothing.

He walked slowly, cautiously, towards the steering cabin, where he had seen the man – the decking planks creaking underneath his rubber-soled shoes. As he approached, he could see several bullet holes in the wall of the cabin.

When he reached the open cabin door, Bernard peered through a small window beside the door and saw the man lying on the floor of the cabin, his eyes still open. In his late twenties, he looked fearfully at Bernard. He was lying in a pool of blood, and apart from small involuntary twitches, appeared to be unable to move. His breathing was shallow and he was gasping in short mouthfuls of air. Next to him lay the AK-47 he'd used to fire at them.

Bernard picked up the battered rifle. Its magazine was detached and it appeared the man had been trying to reload it when he'd gotten shot.

Bernard left the dying man in the steering cabin, and continued his search of the boat. Below deck, he found bunk beds and hammocks for several people. The smell of stale sweat hung in the air. Tattered clothes, dirty plates, and two water jugs with cloudy water still in them were strewn around. It was clear to Bernard that several people had been on the vessel at one stage. *But where were they now?*

He carried on searching, finally reached a storage cabin on the aft deck, where he found blood stains on the floor, and a length of rope that appeared to have been cut through and frayed at the edges. Bernard crouched down and took a closer look at the dried puddle of blood. Close to it, he saw a bent nail in the wall, with a tiny remnant of khaki-coloured fabric caught on the head. Bernard picked it up and rubbed the texture between his fingers. The fabric appeared to be relatively new, as though it hadn't been torn off very long ago

Puzzled, Bernard rose to his feet. He heard Clive's voice from outside.

"Bernard! Come on! We've got company!" Clive sounded panicky.

Once outside, Bernard saw Clive pointing towards the island. In the distance, he saw a small, motorised dinghy, going at full speed, with several men sitting in it. Bernard instinctively crouched down, and lifted his rifle into position. Through the scope, he could see the men more clearly. They were dressed in the same tattered clothes as the man he'd shot. Two of the men wore headbands and one of them had a red bandana tied around his arm.

The dinghy bopped and weaved across the waves, as it hurried towards them.

"Do you see them?" Clive asked unnecessarily.

Bernard nodded and held up one hand to silence Clive. He settled into a kneeling position, and rested his rifle on a wooden crate on the deck. The deeper waters were calm, which gave Bernard the advantage of stabilising his aim.

He waited until the dinghy drew closer, and he could see the men in it were craning their necks, trying to see what was happening on their boat. The dinghy turned slightly, giving Bernard a clear view of all three of the men. He rapid-fired, hitting two of the men almost simultaneously, and then took aim at the third man. The man tried to scramble for cover but it was already too late. Bernard shot him in the back and watched the man fall over in the dinghy.

The dinghy veered off in a different direction, still going at maximum speed but nobody was steering anymore. Bernard stood up to get a clearer view. There was no further movement, and Bernard was confident that the three men on the dinghy were all dead.

40

Jasper and Zelda ran back towards the beach, stopping every few minutes to catch their breath, and to listen and watch for further danger. They knew the remaining men were somewhere ahead of them – they could see their fresh footprints in the sandy soil – but there was a considerable distance to cover. Both of them realised just how far they had run to escape their pursuers – and now they were chasing them!

"This is a really, really, bad idea," Jasper gasped as they stopped for another rest.

"You go back then," said Zelda angrily. "If someone is shooting at these people, then we're on the same side. Maybe they can help us."

For a moment, Jasper weighed up the odds and he considered that going in the opposite direction was probably not a bad idea. *But Zelda might be right,* he thought. This may be a rare chance to get off the island and back to civilisation – to whatever future awaited him there.

He stared at Zelda. Her nakedness seemed completely natural now, and he hardly noticed it at all. Besides, he was too tired and stressed to care.

"Okay, let's do this then," he finally said.

They started to run again, following the trail left by the men. The sun was hot, and there was hardly any breeze on the higher ground. Ironically, it was a perfect day in paradise, Jasper thought.

Minutes later, they reached the top of the hill from where they could see the beach where the men had originally landed. The three remaining men had already reached the dinghy. They were pushing it through the shallow surf and then bundled on board, one of them starting the outboard motor. Moments later, they were on their way, quickly picking up speed and heading towards a larger vessel which lay further offshore.

"Oh my God, look!" said Zelda, pointing at the larger boat. Behind it, they saw a second boat, a gleaming motor yacht. It was half-obscured behind the much older boat.

"It must have been them!" Zelda shouted excitedly. "They did the shooting."

"Maybe we're in the middle of a smuggler's war," Jasper suggested.

Zelda didn't reply.

They watched intently as the dinghy drew closer to the larger boats. The next moment, a number of shots were fired, hitting two of the men in the dinghy, followed by the third. The dinghy veered off in a completely different direction.

"They shot them. They shot all of them..." Jasper said, sounding shocked.

Zelda remained quiet for a moment, then she shouted loudly, waving her arms. "I'm here! Clive! Here!"

"Are you insane?" Jasper said. "They killed those people, and we saw it!" Jasper paused. "Wait, did you just shout 'Clive'?"

Zelda turned to him, her expression serious. "I have a confession," she said, "and I don't have much time."

"Oh my God," Jasper said, realizing what she was about to confess.

"Clive tracked the plane – that's how he knew where to find us," she admitted.

Jasper was incredulous. "You... You knew about this?"

"The kidnapping was... kind of my idea," she said.

"Why? Why would you do that?"

"Payback," she said. "My dear father – I hate that man."

"You hate him that much?"

"More," said Zelda. "He killed the man I wanted to marry."

"Are you... How do you know that?" asked Jasper.

"Listen Jasper," she said. "It was fun and everything, but you have to disappear... now."

"But Clive..."

"Clive will kill you," she said. "I overheard him making plans... to get rid of you when the job was done."

"He can't just..." Jasper started to say, but then he stopped himself. Clive had already demonstrated that he was capable of doing just about anything. "What if they kill you?"

Zelda shook her head. "They won't," she said. "I'm Clive's piggy bank."

"Holy shit," Jasper said, as the reality of the situation sank in.

"I'll tell them you were killed... by those... smugglers," she offered.

She watched Jasper hesitate, struggling with his meagre range of options.

"You'd better go now," she said.

At last, he nodded uncertainly. He retreated, still gripping the AK-47 in his sweaty hands, walking off into the bush, before breaking into a run, putting as much distance as possible between him, Zelda and her accomplices.

41

Zelda descended the steep hill towards the beach below. She was running, stumbling in places, afraid that Clive might depart again, leaving her behind.

Now and again she paused and shouted. "Clive! Wait for me!" She needn't have worried. The motor yacht was already approaching the beach; she could hear its deep rumbling engines as it drew closer.

Finally, she reached the beach. She could see the motor yacht quite clearly now, but just to be sure, she waved her arms and shouted loudly. "Clive! Clive!" The cast on her arm reflected in the sunlight like a beacon.

She could hear the sound of a megaphone crackling, and then she heard Clive's voice. "Zelda! We're coming!"

"Oh thank God!" Zelda shouted. She was exhausted, but relieved.

The water was calm enough to allow the motor yacht to anchor close to the beach. She could see Bernard on the deck, carefully keeping an eye on the water's depth. In the meantime, Clive manoeuvred the motor yacht into position. It slowly swung around, its bow now pointing towards the horizon. The anchor held firm.

Bernard launched an inflatable dinghy off the diving platform at the stern, and tied it in place until Clive clambered aboard.

Within a few minutes, he'd run the dinghy's nose up onto the beach, cut the engine and jumped out.

"Hey honey!" Clive shouted. "Nudist beach, eh?" He smiled broadly.

"Fuck you," she said, smiling with relief. She ran towards him and hugged him fiercely.

Clive squeezed her in a bear hug. "Thank God you're alive, kiddo," he said.

"Please tell me you've got water and good food on that boat."

"Is the Pope Catholic? How well do you know me?" Clive asked with a wide grin.

"Thank God," Zelda said, looking in the direction of the motor yacht in anticipation.

"Where's Monty? Clive asked.

Zelda pulled back out of the hug. She had expected the question. "He didn't make it. The plane crashed... in the water." She kept a poker face, unwilling to tell Clive the rest of the story.

"Where's the pilot?" he asked.

"He didn't make it... either."

Clive watched her suspiciously. A grin slowly spread across his face. "Are you lying to me?" he asked softly.

"For fuck's sake, Clive!"

"A plane goes down, two men die, and you walk away without as much as a scratch... You're laying it on a might thick, don't you think?"

Zelda didn't reply, keeping her gaze determinedly on the large motor yacht. "Alright," she admitted. "The pilot is here... on the island."

"Wait a minute. Did you two... have a little thing?" asked Clive. He watched her reaction carefully, before saying, "Oh God, I didn't think he was your type."

Zelda looked slightly embarrassed. "It was just..." she started. "Listen, he's harmless. Just let him go."

Clive shook his head again, still grinning. "I don't think so, sister. Loose ends, remember?"

"Fuck, he won't say anything. He's scared!" she said.

"He should be, honey. It's time for him to check out."

"I promise you, he won't say a thing."

Clive stared at her without replying.

"Shit," she said, and looked up the hill towards the place where she'd last seen Jasper.

42

Jasper reached the spot where they had left their clothes. The fire had burnt out long before and the ashes were already cold. He dressed hastily, struggling to get his wrinkled pants on one leg at a time.

He looked at Zelda's discarded clothes thoughtfully, and his mind briefly flashed back to their passionate lovemaking the night before. Jasper shook his head, trying to clear it. There was nothing left now, except the hope that he would survive.

When he was dressed, Jasper studied the AK-47 assault rifle. Was it wise to carry it with him? At least if he was unarmed, he could try to talk his way out of trouble – but if he carried the weapon there would be no conversation at all. Still, an AK-47 offered good personal protection. Maybe he could hide it, or perhaps camouflage it, and use it to surprise them...

Jasper doubted that any of his fanciful plans would work, and hoped that Zelda would keep her word and not tell Clive that he was alive. He decided to carry the rifle with him anyway – as insurance, if nothing else.

He headed uphill, walking at a stiff pace. Higher ground; that's where he needed to be right now, he decided. His shirt was unbuttoned, but Jasper was still hot. It was a cloudless day, warm and humid. In no time at all, he was sweating, and wishing that he had a coconut with him, for sustenance.

Jasper ventured into the island's interior, where he thought he'd be safer. Horseflies had stung him on the arms and legs, leaving itchy bumps on his skin. He checked behind him every now and again. There was still no sign of anyone following him.

He stuck to areas with denser vegetation. Occasionally, he caught glimpses of beaches and rocky inlets. Passing one such view, he saw movement near the water. A bare-chested man had emerged from the ocean and quickly crawled across the sand towards the rocks. Moments later the man was out of sight. Jasper blinked a few times, unable to trust his own eyes. *Must be going bonkers!*

He froze and instinctively held his breath, anxiously watching the spot where he had seen the man. but he had disappeared, just as mysteriously as he had appeared. Jasper gripped the AK-47 with both hands and placed his finger on the trigger.

Was it one of Clive's men? Had the man really come ashore without a boat? Was that even possible?

Jasper quietly retreated. He walked briskly in the opposite direction, anxiety flooding his thoughts. What if they were trying to surround him?

He was confused, and losing his sense of direction, but he carried on walking, determined to find a way to safety.

43

From the large window of the Bell 525 helicopter, Jock Speller watched the small tropical island below them. A fishing vessel lay offshore, and there were some people on the beach – visitors from nearby islands, he presumed. Some of them even waved cheerfully at the helicopter as it flew overhead.

Norman Brassington sat opposite him in one of the plush seats. He had headphones on and was listening to some chatter from the local air traffic control towers. Barry, one of the mercenaries they'd hired, sat further towards the back. Floyd was in the co-pilot's seat in the flight deck, and the third member of the team, Nathan, was behind the controls, piloting the helicopter.

The Bell 525 provided all the comfort they needed, and had been fitted with long-range tanks, to limit the need for refuelling stops. The aircraft belonged to an oil-drilling platform, and Jock was able to pull some strings and hire it for a few days without too many questions being asked.

Jock and Norman exchanged looks. They had been flying for several hours, with a single refuelling stop to break the monotony. Jock Speller still looked remarkably fresh, considering the time they had spent on board the aircraft. He had a map in his lap, and was plotting their course to the point where the signal of the floatplane had been lost. He paused now and again to take sips from a bottle of mineral water beside him, and occasionally picked up a pair of field glasses to examine the scenery and the water below them.

Brassington removed his headphones and leaned forward. "What's the plan?" he asked. "When we find the place... do we have a plan?"

Jock too, leant forward. "For you, the plan is to stay out of the line of fire, Norman," he said. "These people know what they're doing."

"You keep telling me that," said Brassington. "I'd still like to know the plan."

As if he was summoned, Floyd entered the cabin through a narrow door from the flight deck. "I trust you are having a pleasant flight, gentlemen," he said with a grin.

"What's the plan?" Brassington repeated the question for Floyd's benefit.

Floyd looked hesitant about discussing his plans with the client, but in the end he acceded. "We do a fly by. If we spot something interesting, we set her down and deploy – we split up. Standard procedure. Scout goes ahead to pinpoint our target, and we move in. Simple as that."

"They could be well armed," Brassington suggested.

"We're well armed," Floyd replied. "And between us, we have the experience to fix any... situation."

Brassington nodded and stared out the window. He was less than convinced by Floyd's answer, but realised that attempting to gain further information from the secretive team would be a waste of time.

The intercom crackled without warning, and they heard Nathan's voice: "Fixer, floating debris in the water. Wanna have a look?"

"Excuse me," Floyd said. 'Fixer' was his nickname in the team. He turned and headed for the flight deck.

Jock Speller peered out of his window and then lifted the field glasses to his eyes. *Finally, something...*

44

Clive Edgewood gave Zelda some of his spare clothes to wear, and as much food and water as she needed. Then he helped Bernard bring some of their supplies ashore.

They were gearing up to walk across the island on foot, so they only carried the essentials – sun hats, insect repellent, light summer clothes, sturdy walking shoes, everything designed to keep them mobile. The water bottles and weapons, on the other hand, added considerably to their pack weight – but that couldn't be helped.

Clive handed Zelda a compact PP-7 pistol. "Just in case," he said. Zelda examined the weapon briefly and then put it in her pocket. "Now can you draw me a picture... of the island?" Clive asked.

Zelda shrugged. "I didn't cover the whole place," she said. "It's big. It sort of extends that way..." she pointed to the northern end of the island.

"Remind me not to ask you for directions," Clive said sarcastically. He looked at Bernard. "Are we ready to go?"

Bernard nodded. "Is he armed?" he asked.

"The pilot?" The thought hadn't occurred to Clive, and he looked at Zelda. "Well? Is he?" When she didn't answer immediately, he continued. "Surely you didn't let him loose with a..."

Zelda bore a pained expression.

"Dear God," Clive said.

"Well, that's a nice touch," Bernard said sarcastically. "What's he carrying?"

Again Clive looked pointedly at Zelda.

"AK-47," she mumbled. When she saw Clive and Bernard exchange glances, she added, "Listen, he doesn't know guns, alright?"

Clive sounded annoyed. "Maybe you haven't been paying attention," he said. "You point the thing and pull the trigger. Bang-bang, we're dead."

"So? We just get on the boat and get out of here. By the time he reaches civilisation again we'll be long gone," said Zelda.

"Doesn't work like that," said Clive. "This thing can come back to bite us – even if it's years down the track."

"Do you have any idea how difficult this has been for me?" Zelda was close to tears.

"We agreed on this and we're going through with it – no matter what," Clive said firmly. "What I need, is for you to stop acting like a schoolgirl and toughen up." Clive turned to Bernard. "What do you think?"

"I agree with you, we need to take him out," said Bernard. "We have to split up – get up onto higher ground and then circle around from two sides. My bet is that he'll try to stay hidden, so he won't come out shooting." He turned to Zelda, his eyes briefly wandering over her now-clothed body. "Maybe you can help to lure him out..."

Zelda didn't respond.

They followed Bernard's plan and headed to higher ground. When they split up, Bernard circled around the northern end of the island, while Clive and Zelda stayed together, taking the southern path. Clive carried an expensive SPAS-12 combat shotgun with a folding stock, which made it quite compact. He carried it by its strap, slung over his shoulder.

Once they were alone, Zelda spoke. "So? Have you got the money?"

Clive shook his head. "Not yet, I had to soften up your old man a bit first... let him stew."

"But everything is going to plan, right?"

"Well, not exactly everything," Clive confessed. "I thought I'd keep Bernard out of this, so I didn't tell him yet, but I've lost contact with Nick."

"What do you mean? I thought—"

"Communication stopped," Clive said. "At some point, he stopped responding, and I couldn't reach him. Probably a technical thing..."

"What if it's not?" Zelda asked.

Clive shook his head. "Nick's smart. If he became aware they were picking up on him, he would have set up somewhere else – relocated the computers, everything, to a new address, and fixed the encryption stuff. He's very cautious. If that's what happened, he would have gone underground for a while, waiting until it was safe to contact me again."

"I hope you're right."

They walked on, picking up the pace.

"Perhaps we shouldn't speak..." said Clive. "Your pilot might hear us."

Zelda nodded glumly, and followed in Clive's footsteps.

45

Jasper felt ridiculous. He had tucked four leafy branches into the belt of his pants, in an attempt to camouflage himself. Glancing down, he could see that his blue shirt was still clearly visible through the leaves.

"Stupid idea," he muttered, and removed the branches. "I'm a dead man, anyway."

He removed the tattered shirt, which had at least been helping to keep the insects at bay, and rolled it in to a tight ball, carrying it in one hand. For a moment, he considered removing his pants too, but decided against it. If he was going to die, he would die with dignity, he thought.

He picked up the AK-47 and walked on, looking for the most densely wooded areas in which to hide – somewhere to hide until nightfall. *But what then?*

Jasper decided he couldn't worry about the next step, or the next. What he needed now, was to find a good hiding spot. A few minutes later, he found a promising possibility – shaded by a tree, with a large rock on one side shielding him from view.

He crawled into the narrow opening between the rock and the tree, and found a reasonably comfortable place on the sandy soil where he could park himself.

He wriggled into a more-or-less comfortable position, and with the AK-47 clasped in his hands, Jasper leaned against the rock, appreciating its coolness. Then he settled down for a long wait.

46

The helicopter flew at extremely low altitude, about a hundred metres above the waves. It allowed Floyd, in the co-pilot's seat, to do a high-speed scan of the water below them, searching for more signs of aircraft debris.

Nathan was steering them towards the nearest large island. Satisfied that they had found parts of the floatplane in the water, they were now searching for the survivors.

The island was surprisingly close, and as they approached, Nathan increased their altitude in preparation for a first fly-by.

Floyd's voice crackled over the internal radio. "Two boats at ten o'clock," he said. "Let's check them out."

Nathan gave him a crisp nod and dipped the helicopter's nose towards the beach. They saw a large, luxury motor yacht gleaming in the afternoon sun, and a rickety fishing vessel anchored further offshore.

The helicopter slowed to a hover near the motor yacht, its five-bladed rotor whipping up a white froth on the water. They were so close they could read the name printed on the stern: *Silver Tambourine*.

"That's it!" Floyd's voice was louder and he sounded excited. "Can you see anyone on board?"

Nathan shook his head, concentrating on keeping the helicopter hovering near the yacht.

"Take us once around the island. They know we're here now. No more secrets," said Floyd with a grin. "Barry?"

"Ready," the third member of the team replied over the internal radio.

In the cabin, Barry had been strapped into the seat closest to the door. He released his seatbelt, unzipped a duffel bag and withdrew a G-36 assault rifle, briefly checking the magazine. Satisfied, he leaned towards the window and peered out.

The helicopter had gained height and flew over the island, several sets of eyes scanning the bushes on the ground below them.

From his seat, Jock was also staring out through the window, and listened intently for further directions on his earphones. This was it. His pulse raced. He glanced over at Norman Brassington, but Norman ignored him, searching out of his own window. The man still held the whiskey glass which he'd sipped from regularly throughout the flight. His face showed no emotion.

They flew around the northern end of the island first. The noise scared a few seabirds into hasty flight, but other than that they saw no movement on the ground.

They circled around to the southern end of the island, approaching from a distance at first, then swooping in and flying low above the trees. The wave of air from the powerful rotor blades rippled across the tree tops and bushes, disturbing the tranquillity of the scene.

Then Floyd saw it – a quick movement in the bushes; so fast that he nearly missed it. It was high up on a ridge, in a cluster of bushes. "There!" he said loudly over the internal communications system.

Nathan followed his command almost immediately. The helicopter hung like an airborne insect, hungrily searching for its prey, nose downwards and mere metres above the tree tops.

But their prey had escaped, or so it seemed. Whoever Floyd had seen was no longer visible, but he was quite certain he had spotted someone.

"Find a place to land," he barked out.

The helicopter retreated, gaining altitude as Nathan searched for a suitable landing spot. It was difficult terrain; bushy, steep slopes and rocky shores. They were going to have to have to fly back towards the nearest beach to land safely.

Floyd didn't want to give his quarry time to escape. "Do a low drop, Nathe," he said, and pointed to a level area near the rocks. The area was too small to land, but at least it was a possible drop spot.

Sea breezes turned into sudden gusts against the southern side of the island, and it took considerable skill to guide the large helicopter towards the rocky area, where large breakers foamed and sea spray shot up into the air. Nathan released the landing gear and hovered low, while Floyd disappeared into the cabin to strap on his backpack and open the sliding hatch.

They were still metres above the ground – too high to make the jump. Floyd and Barry waited until the helicopter's wheels were almost touching the rocks below them, and then they jumped, hitting the rocky surface hard, and rolling to reduce the impact on their bodies.

Barry suffered a jarring impact in his left leg. He grabbed his injured leg, grimacing as pains shot up into his thigh and pelvis. Then he stumbled to his feet, groaning loudly. The assault rifle tumbled out of his hands and clattered onto the rock.

"Stay low!" Floyd shouted above the noise of the helicopter, but his warning came too late.

A single shot echoed from high on the hill and Barry was thrown violently backward, his blood spraying over the rock. Floyd dove for cover, and frantically tried to signal Nathan to leave immediately.

Another two shots rang out, both of them penetrating the steel bodywork near the helicopter's engine. On the flight deck the sound resembled two loud twangs.

"Get out of here!" Floyd shouted from the ground. It was clear the sniper was trying to disable the helicopter.

Even though Floyd knew Nathan couldn't hear him, it became apparent that Nathan realized the danger they were in. The helicopter lifted and then tilted its nose forward, rapidly picking up speed. Within a matter of seconds, if was heading out over the waves, making it difficult for the shooter to do any further damage.

On the ground, Floyd crawled along underneath the sparse cover provided by the bushes, until he reached the rock where Barry lay. He crawled around it, while checking on his comrade.

"Barry!" he shouted. Then louder: "Barry!"

The man was still alive, but his voice was racked with pain. "Sniper," he groaned. "On the hill."

"I saw him," Floyd replied. "Can you move?"

Floyd saw the minute shake of his head.

"I'm going get you off the rock!" shouted Floyd. "Understand?"

Barry groaned a response, one that Floyd couldn't quite make out.

"I'm coming to get you!" said Floyd. "Get ready!"

Seconds later, Floyd jumped up and grabbed hold of Barry's backpack. He pulled hard, trying to pull his friend into the protected area behind the rock. Barry was a dead weight in his arms, and it took all of Floyd's strength to move him a few inches.

Barry groaned loudly, managing to roll over onto his stomach. He clawed at the rock, trying to assist Floyd by crawling forward.

Another shot rang out, hitting Barry in the thigh. The impact shook his body and shattered his femur. He howled in pain.

"Son of a bitch!" Floyd growled, withdrawing behind of the rock. "Barry?" he yelled. "Can you hear me?"

Barry sobbed. Fear and intense pain had overwhelmed him, and he was no longer able to respond.

"Two more inches, Barry!" Floyd shouted. "Crawl forward two more inches, and I can help you."

There was no response, except for more sobs and groans.

Floyd flicked off the safety on his rifle. He took a few quick breaths, steadied himself on his haunches and settled his back against the rock. A moment later, he rose up, swung around and took aim at the top of the hill where he'd seen the sniper's muzzle flash. He fired a quick burst of shots, then grabbed Barry's backpack, and pulled as hard as he could. Barry's body slid towards him slowly, and he kept dragging until it reached the edge of the rock and tumbled down behind it.

Floyd ducked out of sight, and tried to help his fallen comrade. Blood was streaming out of Barry's mouth and nostrils, and gurgling noises sounded in his throat, as if he was drowning in his own blood.

Floyd knew then that it was too late to save him.

47

Zelda managed to stop herself from screaming when the first shots were fired. Her eyes grew wide with fear. She and Clive had crawled into the undergrowth together, and were now lying side by side, staring anxiously at one another. They had heard Barry's groans, and they sounded uncomfortably close to their position.

"Holy Jesus, they're going to kill us all," Zelda whispered loudly, and bit back her tears.

"They won't kill *you*," Clive whispered back.

"You don't know what my father's capable of—" she began.

Clive shushed her as he listened to the sound of the helicopter. It was moving further away.

"What do we do now?" said Zelda.

Clive was still breathing rapidly, but quietly congratulated himself for offering Bernard the job. He realised that Bernard had saved him from certain death. "They spotted us from the chopper. I'm sure of it," he said to Zelda. "We can't stay here."

"We can't run," said Zelda, fear rising in her voice.

Clive shook his head. "Not run, crawl. We need to put some distance between us and them."

"Which way?"

"This way," he said and began crawling, flat on his belly. He paused for a moment and looked back at Zelda. "Stay low, for God's sake."

"Do I look like an idiot?" Even in her moments of high anxiety, Zelda was never at a loss for words.

They crawled as quietly as possible, their bellies scraping over stones and when their clothes caught on dry branches, the silence was broken by the sound of the wood snapping. These sudden bursts of noise stopped them in their tracks, holding their breath, but not for long. There was a long way to go, and no time to waste.

At the top of the hill, Bernard changed his position. From experience, he knew that it was wiser to give up his location at the top of the hill, even though it was a prime area. He had been spotted, and they would soon be coming for him. Keeping to the high ground, he moved in a direction away from the beach, as it was reasonable to assume the helicopter would bring reinforcements.

Behind the cover of the hill, he could move faster, and he managed to make good ground in a few short minutes. Then he spotted another good position – a half-circle of rocks, which offered the additional benefit of having medium-sized bushes growing around it. He could use the rocks as protective cover, and remain almost entirely hidden behind the bushes.

He crawled into his new hiding place, and checked his magazine and rifle. He was certain he wouldn't have long to wait.

48

Floyd removed the contents from Barry's backpack, and added most of it to his own. The sniper wouldn't remain in one position for too long, and Floyd estimated that he had a couple of minutes to seek a better, less-exposed position.

He crawled out from behind the rock and used the cover of the nearby bushes to make his way further up the hill, moving forward cautiously and keeping a sharp lookout.

Before long, he'd successfully disappeared into a densely vegetated area. He stopped for a moment, switched on the tiny two-way radio that he carried on his belt, and pressed an earbud into his ear.

He tapped out a silent code on the radio, and moments later received a response from the helicopter. The chopper had landed, and Nathan was ready to receive fresh orders.

49

Jasper had been sitting in the same cramped position for what seemed like an eternity, and he'd finally decided to stand up to stretch his legs when he heard the approaching helicopter. He swiftly returned to his hiding place, and frantically covered himself with branches, before the helicopter passed overhead. Not long afterwards, he'd heard the shots, and he remained frozen in fear, completely confused about what was going on around him.

Now that the shooting was over, it had grown eerily quiet.

He was lying as still as possible, almost too afraid to breathe, when he realised he'd completely forgotten about the AK-47! He'd propped it up against a tree while he'd been stretching his legs.

Jasper cursed himself for being so careless, and for abandoning his hiding spot in the first place.

He lifted his head slowly, peering past his hastily-assembled camouflage, and could see the rifle exactly where he'd left it. He caught a flash of sudden movement from the corner of his eye, but the moment he turned to look, it was gone. *An animal, perhaps, or a bird?* Jasper's heart pounded in his chest. If it was a man, it could only have been an enemy.

Jasper tried to remain very still. His breathing sounded like the puffing of a steam engine inside his head.

He squeezed his eyes closed, willing himself to remain absolutely still, and to take control of the panic that had gripped his entire body. This method seemed to work, albeit slowly. His breathing slowed slightly, and the feeling of panic resettled down into his stomach, forming a solid knot in his gut.

When he reopened his eyes, dappled sunlight was warming his face. The branch that he had hastily arranged to cover his head created a broken picture of the sky above him. He lay quietly and listened. Apart from bird noises and the distant sound of the ocean, he could hear nothing except his own breathing.

He slowly, painfully slowly, raised his head and looked around. Everything was exactly as before, and relief washed over him. But then he looked in the direction of the tree where he had left the AK-47. It was gone!

Impossible!

It was simply not possible for an automatic rifle to disappear into thin air, thought Jasper – and the panic flooded his nervous system. His single chance of survival had been snapped away from under his nose. Jasper was trembling uncontrollably, and for a long moment he was certain he was going to pee in his pants.

What the hell? Who could have taken it?

For a moment, Jasper experienced a bizarre vision of the local wildlife – *maybe a large rat?* — dragging the AK-47 along the ground. Was he losing his mind? Is this how people went crazy? The thoughts and images whirled through his mind – and his breathing grew erratic, coming out in short bursts. He began to pray that his brain would simply shut down, and he would mercifully float off into an unconscious state.

But it didn't happen.

Jasper thought he heard movement in the bushes – as if someone was creeping through the dense branches. A rustle of leaves here, the snap of a twig there... Was it coming towards him, or moving away? He couldn't decide. Did it matter? Jasper suspected he was already wearing a dead man's clothes. He simply had to wait for the fateful moment – when someone put him out of his misery.

He raised his head again. It had gone suddenly quiet. Whoever, or whatever, was creating the noise had disappeared. For Jasper, the separation between dream and sleep, between imagination and reality, had blurred. He sat upright, removed the branch that was perched almost comically on top of his head, and again looked at the spot where he'd left the AK-47. Did he ever carry the AK-47 at all? Jasper began to doubt his own memories.

He sat upright, aware of a stiffness that had settled into his joints. What was he supposed to do now, when he was utterly defenceless?

He decided to get to his feet, peer through the bushes – and discover what was out there.

50

Norman Brassington and Jock Speller elected to stay behind on the beach, leaving it to Nathan to take the helicopter on a reconnaissance flight – with instructions from Floyd to spot and, if possible, flush out the sniper.

Jock and Norman headed towards a rocky outcrop near the beach, where they could take shelter. They were both armed, each man carrying a pistol. Jock also had an automatic rifle slung over his shoulder, and he carried some spare ammunition and an emergency medical kit.

They heard the ascending whine of the engines, and watched as the helicopter took off. It turned sharply and headed towards the northern tip of the island, flying low. After a few minutes it disappeared behind the hills, leaving only a faint echo of the chip-chip-chip as the blades cut through the air.

Norman Brassington still stared at the sky, even though the helicopter was no longer visible. "What if they fuck the whole thing up?" he said, his voice rough and hoarse. "What if they don't get those bastards?"

Jock shook his head. "They won't fail. They're trained professionals."

Norman looked at him, his eyes bleary from drinking way too much whiskey on the flight. "And what if they do fail? Are you up for it?" He lifted the hand that held the pistol, and waved it around.

"Of course," said Jock grimly. "We won't stop until we find her." A sense of melancholy had settled over him. Had his entire life really come down to this?

"Finding her is not enough," Norman said quietly. "I want the scum obliterated. I want to hit them so hard, it will feel like a religious experience when they die. And you think this mob is up to it?"

"They're the best chance we've got," Jock replied.

Norman spat on the sand. It was the most descriptive reply he could muster.

51

The Bell 525 flew behind and along the rocky ridge at the top of the hills. Nathan wanted to dampen the noise and disguise his approach as much as possible. It also put him in a position to spot the sniper if he was still at the top of the hills.

Nathan knew he was dealing with an experienced shooter, and that it would be very difficult for him to spot a single figure hiding in the bushes, but at least the vegetation at the top of the hills was sparser, so it provided fewer hiding spots.

His flight path hugged the hillside, and his eyes were locked onto the ground that passed rapidly beneath him. But there was no sign of movement and no clues as to the whereabouts of the sniper. It was clear the shooter was in hiding, waiting for an opportune moment.

Nathan flew to the northern tip of the island, turned, and headed back along the southern ridge, his body tense and his hands locked tightly onto the dual flight controls. In front of him, the electronic screens glowed green and blue, and the artificial horizon shifted rapidly as he flew closer and then further away from the hill.

A moment later, he spotted the tiniest of movements behind a small clump of rocks. Two seconds later, a loud crack made him jump. A bullet had hit the flight deck window, and left a small hole which sucked out the air. Nathan instinctively turned the helicopter away, heading seaward. He heard several more shots hitting the body of the Bell 525.

An alarm sounded on the flight deck. There was a sudden and dramatic loss of oil pressure – the oil cooler had been hit. Nathan yanked the yoke to one side and the helicopter veered dangerously. He had no choice now but to head back to the beach, as fast as he could.

He immediately contacted Floyd by radio and, through a crackle of electricity, described the place where he had seen the sniper.

52

"He hit the chopper," Clive whispered loudly to Zelda. "Bernard hit the chopper." He was excited, elated. Finally, things were going their way.

Zelda felt his excitement, but she looked worried. "Clive, my father will never give up. He'll see us all dead first. You don't know him."

"I spoke to him on the phone, remember? He's just human. He'll give up eventually. You'll see."

"He'll destroy the boat. There will be no way for us to get off this fucking island. I'm serious," she muttered.

"Not if we hit them first..." said Clive. He lifted his shotgun.

"What? What are you thinking?" asked Zelda.

Clive ignored her question. "Follow me," he said urgently. He scrambled to his feet and peeked out of their hiding place among the bushes.

"Keep down," Zelda warned.

But Clive was already dashing through the bushes, running towards the northern tip of the island, and away from the spot where the helicopter had dropped off the other two men. After a moment's indecision, Zelda stood up and sprinted after him – only to see Clive take a tumble and fall down heavily.

She heard him swear loudly. "I hate this place!" Clive growled, getting back on his feet.

Clive glanced back at Zelda, but then he turned his head slightly and was looking past her, further up the hill. "Shit!" he shouted, and swung the shotgun into a firing position. But it was already too late. Someone else fired first, hitting Clive twice in the stomach and once in the leg. The force of the shots flung Clive backwards, and the shotgun fell out of his hands.

Zelda screamed, and watched in horror as Clive, drenched in blood, crawled towards the shotgun. The other man moved in quickly, lifted his rifle and shot again, this time hitting Clive in the arm. Then he ducked out of sight.

Clive's body was gripped by spasms. His muscles contracted and he curled up involuntarily. He groaned loudly, trying to breathe through mouthfuls of blood.

"Get down if you want to live!" The other man shouted at Zelda.

Zelda obeyed instantly. She ducked to the ground and remained there, hiding among the bushes.

She heard the man speaking again. "Stay there. I'll come get you when this is over."

Zelda nodded frantically, even though she knew the other man couldn't see her.

She remained motionless, shivering with fear and hardly moving a muscle. She could hear Clive, who lay just metres away, groaning weakly. He was still alive.

Zelda inched forward on her stomach, worming her way through the tall grass.

"Clive...?" she whispered, but there was no response.

She found him, minutes later, and was shocked at the amount of blood pooling around him.

His eyes were wide open, and stricken with pain. Blood flowed freely from his mouth.

He parted his lips, but no words came out. He shaped his lips to form the word 'kiddo'. It was meaningless to Zelda.

Zelda's eyes glistened with tears. "Baby..." she whispered.

Clive appeared to be grinning slightly, or maybe he was just grimacing. She saw his body sag, and realised this was the end for him.

His shotgun lay in the grass, about four metres away. Zelda began slowly crawling towards it.

53

Bernard had expected to see his quarry emerge from the bushes, but he was surprised when the man suddenly stood up and fired several shots. He knew instantly that Clive had been hit, and swung his rifle towards Clive's shooter, but before he could lock on to his target, the man ducked under cover and disappeared.

Bernard swept the area with his rifle scope but there was no sign of the other man. He was using the dense bushes to his advantage.

Bernard knew he was up against an experienced adversary. Being a cautious fighter, he decided to dig in and wait for his opponent to make the first move.

Floyd was inching forward on his belly, pushing his rifle ahead of him while trying to minimise the noise he made. He knew the sniper would be waiting and anything – from the rustling of leaves to the slightest movement of a branch – would give him away. But he did have a vague sense of where the sniper was hiding, based on Nathan's directions.

He reached a rocky outcrop and was able to pick up speed by moving forward on all fours. He felt the buzzing of the two-way radio in his pocket, and stopped to check it.

The LCD read: 'Chopper fucked. Reached the beach OK'.

Floyd tapped out a coded message to Nathan. 'Stay there. One down. Hunting other.'

He received a short reply in return: 'R'. *Roger.*

Floyd was certain that he was up against a single opponent – the sniper. Now it was down to the painstaking task of tracking him down and flushing him out. He regretted not having the benefit of a grenade, but put his regrets aside and focused on the task ahead. He estimated the sniper was within easy range of his rifle, but realised that he would be well hidden and waiting for him. Weighing his options, Floyd decided to crawl across towards the northern end of the hill, keeping a look-out for any movement, anything that would betray the sniper.

He began edging his way forward, clutching the rifle close, while keeping his elbows free to leopard-crawl forward. It was painfully slow, but lessened the risk of being spotted.

Bernard shifted slightly to improve the blood circulation in his arms and legs. He was well positioned, with rocks protecting him on most sides, and trees providing a good canopy under which to hide, especially if his opponent was higher on the hill.

He heard a tiny rustling sound and froze, slowly turning his head in the direction of the noise, his fingers tightening around the rifle grip. The rustling didn't repeat itself, but it did manage to put him further on edge. He sniffed the air like an animal, and analysed every little sound within his defence perimeter. The sounds of the distant waves breaking on to the rocks were filtered out, and the sounds nearer to him amplified in his mind.

Even the most experienced snipers knew that this level of high alert could not be maintained indefinitely. Sooner or later, the human brain demanded release, so the trick was to relax your guard and then resume it again after a few minutes of relief. Bernard knew this. He relaxed, breathing easier again for a while.

He heard the unmistakable sound of approaching footsteps. The person was trying to move quietly, but in the process crushed little twigs and dried grasses underfoot. The footsteps were clear to anyone as focused on the noise as Bernard was. He sat quietly, not moving a muscle, until the footsteps came closer. Someone was approaching from an unexpected direction, and Bernard mapped this movement in his head, carefully judging the distance.

The next moment, he unwound like a snake – lightning fast – and swung the rifle around at the approaching sound. He glimpsed something at the corner of his eye – from the opposite side. *What? Two people approaching?*

Before he had the chance to react, he was hit in the shoulder, and in the next instant he heard the fire of an automatic weapon, and a woman's scream from nearby. *Zelda!*

Several other bullets ricocheted off the rocks around him. He could see movement – a man, running – and Bernard lifted his rifle instinctively, oblivious to the blood that was oozing out of his shoulder and the searing pain that accompanied it. He fired blindly – twice, three times – and saw the man fall down. It was the one he had been waiting for.

Bernard's high-velocity bullet hit the other man in the side, shattering his rib and travelling on, rupturing his heart, and exiting at the other end, leaving a gaping wound and killing him before he even hit the ground. The man's body collapsed in a heap, his limbs sprawled, and his face ended up half-buried in the sandy soil.

Bernard was breathing rapidly. He was abruptly aware of the intense pain emanating from the wound in his shoulder. The bullet had passed through, but left a large open wound. It was bleeding profusely. Bernard tried to move his arm but found that it hung like a dead weight from his shoulder, making the pain even worse. His rifle lay uselessly at his side.

"Holy shit!" he heard. It was Zelda's voice. "Holy shit, don't shoot, I'm begging you!" she cried out.

Bernard could hear her clearly, but couldn't see her. She was crying, almost hysterically, and seemed to be wandering aimlessly.

"Stay down..." Bernard tried to say, but the words came out as a hoarse whisper. He was aware of a hissing noise in his chest.

Zelda stumbled over loose stones, and stepped forward as if she was walking in a dream. A few metres ahead she saw a stranger's body, lying motionless on the ground. She lifted the shotgun and aimed at the limp figure, but there was no movement. It was clear he was dead.

She turned, peering around with teary eyes. "Bernard...?" she whispered. And then more loudly. "Bernard?"

She heard a groan, and stepped cautiously in the direction of the sound. "Don't you shoot," she warned.

There was no response; just the sound of the sea and the squawk of a bird in the distance.

"Bernard," she said again, continuing to walk forward. She discovered Bernard slumped against a rock, his face pale and his breathing shallow. He looked up as she approached. His grimace almost resembled a smile.

"He got me," he said.

"Fuck," said Zelda. "Clive is dead."

Bernard nodded imperceptibly.

Zelda surveyed their surroundings, then moved closer to Bernard. He was clearly not in a good state. His shoulder was badly shot up, and he was losing a lot of blood. "Who else?" she asked.

"The chopper," Bernard said, groaning with pain. "The others are at the chopper."

"They'll come for us," said Zelda fearfully.

"Help me up," Bernard said. "We need to... hide." His face was distorted with pain.

Zelda was still looking around, afraid that the others might be close.

"It will take them awhile..." Bernard panted, "to get here."

Zelda stared at his wound in increasing horror.

He lifted his gaze to her. "Help me." He attempted to lift his good arm, to reach out to her.

Zelda sniffed and wiped the tears from her eyes. "You can't fight them," she said. "Not like this."

"Just get me up," he said. "We'll figure out something..." But then he noticed Zelda's strange look. "Get me up, will you?" He propped himself up, trying to sit up straight. "Zelda?"

Zelda shook her head.

"What?"

She looked anguished. "I can't help you," she admitted slowly.

"What are you—?" he began to speak, but Zelda shook her head.

"Fuck it," she whispered.

"Zelda," Bernard pleaded. "Listen—"

"I can't carry you. I can't help you," she said.

"You're just going to leave me?"

Zelda sniffed loudly, and lifted the shotgun up to her shoulder.

"Hey! I helped you," Bernard said, his voice suddenly loud and desperate.

Zelda just shook her head.

"They'll come looking for me, maybe in a day or two," she said. "It may slow them down if they can't recognise you."

"What the fuck are you—?" Her intentions suddenly became clear to Bernard. "No!" he cried. "Don't you—"

The sound of the shot was deafening. Zelda's shot hit Bernard in the face, instantly obliterating it.

54

"He's not responding," Nathan said, still clutching the small two-way radio in his hands. "I checked all our frequencies."

Jock looked worried, and he stared towards the northern end of the island, where the sound of gunfire had come from.

"Mister Brassington and I will bunker down here," Jock said finally. "You'd better go see if you can find Floyd – and whoever else is left."

Nathan nodded. He slipped on his backpack and picked up his assault rifle. With a final glance at Jock Speller and Norman Brassington, he set off across the beach, heading north at a brisk pace.

"To hell in a handbasket." Jock heard Brassington's voice behind him. He turned to see the big man staring at him with a grin on his face. "Can't really describe this one as a runaway fucking success, can we?"

Jock ignored his statement. "We must find you a safe place, in case…" he said.

"You're baby-sitting me now? I'm disappointed, Jock. Give me some credit, will you?" Brassington patted the pistol that he'd stuck into his belt. "If they want me, they can fucking come get me."

"Floyd shot one of them," Jock said. "But the other one may have escaped."

"Which means he's trigger happy and almost certainly will come after us," said Brassington, still grinning.

"Maybe."

"What about the chopper?" asked Brassington. "Can he fix it?"

"Nathan said he'll look at it," Jock replied.

Brassington spat on the sand. "I hate boats," he said, looking at the motor yacht anchored offshore.

Jock was suddenly angry at his boss. "It will be more helpful if you are... cooperative," he said.

Brassington gave a dry chuckle. "Worried are we?" he said. "Don't want your family to know you died on some piss-willy, god-forsaken island? What's left of my family is right here, Jock. Somewhere in that bush. One happy family, all together."

"I'm sorry," said Jock. "I'm concerned for your safety, that's all."

"Fuck my safety. And fuck yours. We're settling this thing today," said Norman.

55

Nathan's fitness paid off. He started at a brisk walking pace, before breaking into a jog and ascending the hill with relative ease. His boots kicked up sand as he wound his way up the natural pathways further up the hill.

He held the G-36 assault rifle in one hand, and his backpack was as light as he could make it – which allowed him to keep moving forward at a good speed. He realised it was important to complete the job before sunset, as the night would bring additional risks. Still, it was difficult to determine exactly what 'the job' was. Nathan guessed the sniper was still out there and waiting for him. Floyd, he assumed, was out of the game – either wounded or dead. Then there was the girl, if she was still alive. It was now up to him to swing the balance in his favour.

In spite of the heat, Nathan remained light on his feet, although by the time he reached the highest point on the nearest hill, he was sweating profusely. After twenty minutes, he stopped and drank some water. He used the opportunity to scan the area with a pair of small, but powerful field glasses, but there was nothing to capture his interest.

Keeping to the cover provided by a rocky ridge near the top of the hill, he moved on, making good time as he moved to the northern tip of the island. He estimated it would take him at least another half an hour to reach the spot where he had seen Floyd.

56

Jasper Owen put as much distance between himself and the sound of gunfire as possible. He retreated to the northern tip of the island, taking cover every few minutes by diving under bushes, and crawling along for metres at a stretch.

He was exhausted, his elbows bleeding from crawling over rough terrain, and his nerves were wound so tight that he suspected his mind would snap at any moment.

He felt as if he was ready to lie down on the ground and die. There was little hope of survival for him anyway, he reasoned.

He stopped, this time resting with his back against a tree, and looked out to sea. Maybe he could swim, he thought – just swim out to sea and hope that he would be spotted by a boat. He dismissed the idea instantly, realising just how stupid it sounded. It was obvious that he would drown, long before any boat would be able to reach him.

His legs trembled, and Jasper knew that he was close to collapse, but he refused to sit down. *Sit down and die? Here? Never!*

He stubbornly remained standing and forced himself to consider his options. He could remain where he was and stay hidden; or go back on his tracks in the hope that his hunters were no longer following him; or traverse to the opposite end of the island.

In his fevered mind, the last option made the most sense. At least that way, he would keep moving, instead of sitting down and pondering the thousands of ways in which his life could come to a brutal end.

Scraping together the last of his energy resources, Jasper moved on. His decision made him feel better, more confident. For a moment, he even felt a tiny bit of optimism, which quickly blossomed into a sense of excitement. *What if survival was possible after all?*

For almost half an hour, he scrambled over rocks, waded through pools of water, and stumbled through bushy terrain until he reached an area that was clearer and easier to navigate. It was a relief to escape the tangled branches he had left behind, and Jasper was about to sit down to rest when he caught a small movement from the corner of his eye.

On a rock, a mere few metres away, a man was sitting and watching him. He had an assault rifle in his hands, which he casually lifted and aimed at Jasper's head.

"And you are?" the man said. His voice was soft, but Jasper caught every syllable, as if the man was inside his head.

Jasper sunk to his knees, and stared at the ground in front of him. So this is how it was going to end. Shot in the head, without ceremony.

Half of him wanted to throw up. The other half wanted to simply curl up and die – to deny the man the pleasure of killing him.

"Who are you?" the man asked sharply.

Jasper shook his head. "Nobody," he said, and then added: "The pilot. I'm the pilot."

"Where are the others?"

Jasper lifted a hand, but let it drop almost instantly. "I don't know. Shooting. I don't know... what happened," he said, his voice hoarse from exhaustion.

"You ran away?"

"No," said Jasper. "Yes..." He gave a weak nod.

"Do you know who's still alive?" the man prodded.

Jasper looked up at him, as if he was asking a ludicrous question, and shook his head.

The man with the rifle stood up slowly, almost lazily. "You're coming with me," he said.

Jasper dropped his head and shook it from side to side.

"If you want to live, you'll come with me," the man repeated. He moved towards Jasper, keeping a safe distance between them. Then he switched the safety off on his assault rifle. "It's your call."

57

Zelda left the two dead men, and the shotgun, at the scene of the shooting and began walking back to the beach to meet her father and his henchmen. *After all, there was precious little choice now,* she thought.

The image of Bernard's face, frozen in surprise, moments before it was transformed into a bloody mess, remained in her mind while she walked. She felt empty, and without remorse. *We all take our chances.*

Zelda walked slowly, unconsciously trying to delay the inevitable. It took several minutes for her rational mind to kick into gear. There was a still a chance that her father knew nothing about her part in the staged kidnapping – a chance that she could walk off scot free. The thought of it put her in a slightly better mood, and for the first time she appreciated the beautiful sea view.

In a moment of weird detachment, Zelda wondered if she was in a dream. The sea took on an unusual green colour, and the sound of the waves faded into the background. Instead, her ears picked up a different sound: she could hear her own name, carried on a light breeze.

Someone was calling her name!

Zelda glanced behind her, half-expecting to see Bernard following her. But the voice came from the top of a ridge, from higher ground. She looked up and saw Jasper, stumbling forward and making his way down the hill. Then she saw the stranger behind him. He was carrying a rifle – one of her father's henchmen.

Zelda stopped and stared at the two men as they approached. She felt cheated. It was rather disappointing that good daydreams were always so short.

It took the two men several minutes to reach her over the rough terrain. Zelda waited patiently, and made no effort to close the distance between them. *Jasper was still alive!*

She absent-mindedly touched the PP-7 pistol in her pocket. Even if she could do it, Zelda knew it would be fruitless to remove the man with the rifle. There would be others waiting – with her father – she was certain of it.

"Zelda!" Jasper called again, much closer now.

She looked up, staring impassively at him.

"With the shooting... I thought you were..." he said, as he approached. The man with the rifle said nothing, and Zelda sensed that he was aware of the pistol she had in her pocket.

Jasper lapsed into silence when she didn't respond, glancing back at the man behind him.

"You're Zelda Brassington?" the man with the rifle asked, and Zelda nodded. "Your father is waiting," he added.

Zelda nodded again.

"I want you to hand over your weapon," he said. "For your own safety."

Zelda gave him a bruised look. "For my own safety? Bullshit! It stays with me," she said.

Zelda and the man with the rifle locked eyes in a brief stare-off, before he finally relented. "Fine," he said. "We're heading that way." He gestured in a southerly direction with the barrel of his assault rifle, then prodded Jasper to start walking by pressing the muzzle into his back. Jasper meekly followed the path back towards the beach.

"What happened… to the others?" Jasper finally asked.

Zelda shot him a poisoned glance. "Let's not speak," she said, and walked ahead of him, leading the way.

She heard Jasper speaking to the man with the rifle. "I was just the pilot. I was duped, I swear. You can ask her," he said.

The man's response was blunt. "Keep walking."

"They never told me what—" Jasper began, but he was cut short by Zelda.

"Oh for fuck's sake, will you shut up?" she spat out.

Jasper walked on in silence.

58

Jock spotted them first.

"They're coming," he said briefly to Norman Brassington, while watching the approaching party with binoculars.

Brassington frowned, taking the binoculars from Jock and peering through the lenses. The image was clear, and digitally enhanced, giving him a perfect view even though the threesome was still a considerable distance away.

"Well, at least someone has come to work today," he muttered, and handed the field glasses back to Jock.

"I'm guessing the other man is the pilot," Jock suggested.

"Our man should have shot him, and saved us the bother."

"He might have information..."

Brassington spat on the ground. He bent down and took a revolver from a holster that lay on top of one of the duffel bags they'd off-loaded from the helicopter. "Might do the job myself," he mumbled.

They stood waiting for a tense twenty minutes while the others approached. Zelda walked in front, and slowed down when they reached the beach, trudging through soft sand.

"Norman," said Jock after a long silence. "It's not my place to tell you what to say to your daughter…"

"Then don't," Brassington snapped.

Jock opened his mouth to protest, but quickly realised there was little sense in it. He just shook his head instead. He had never seen Brassington in such a dark mood.

When Zelda came closer, Jock noticed that her clothes were smudged with brown stains, and her hair was an unkempt mop. Despite the tension, he grinned. He remembered her teenage years, and the fiery arguments she had had with her dad. Try as he might, Norman had been unable to tame his daughter.

Jock wanted to walk towards her, but Brassington stopped him: "Stay there." His voice was deep and gravelly.

Jock was puzzled, and stared at the man for whom he had worked for more than twenty years. "You got what you wanted," he said, but big Norman ignored him.

"Zelda," Jock said, as they got closer. "Thank God you're alive." He wanted to walk towards her and hug her, but he held back. It was Brassington's stage.

Zelda came to a halt. Jasper stopped behind her, obviously trying to keep her as a shield between him and Brassington, who carried the look of a wounded bear.

Nathan made his way to Jock Speller's side and spoke softly. "He's the pilot," he said. "Floyd is… out of commission."

"What are you speaking to him for?" Brassington growled at Nathan. "I'm in charge here."

Jock nodded at Nathan, encouraging him to obey.

Nathan slowly moved over to Brassington's side, but the big man ignored him, as if he didn't want to hear his report at all.

Brassington took a step forward and looked at Zelda. "You've fucked up for the last time," he said.

"I was kidnapped," she retorted angrily.

"And who came up with that sterling plan? I won't believe a single thing you say, you little bitch. You caused this!" he bellowed.

Jock interrupted: "We... we questioned the man who—"

"Shut up!" Brassington shouted. "I will deal with this."

"Deal with this? That's rich! You're the fucking pig who killed my fiancé!" Zelda shouted back. Then, more subdued, she added. "Dane should still have been alive today."

"That arsehole was soaked in drugs. We just helped him on his way," Brassington snapped.

"So you admit it?"

"The slime was after your money, that's all. He got the easy way out." Brassington's voice had taken on a low and more menacing tone.

"That's all I needed to know," Zelda said. She withdrew the pistol from her pocket, before Brassington and Jock had a chance to react.

Nathan did react. He lifted his rifle, and Zelda responded instantaneously – she fired, shooting him in the eye. Nathan fell backwards onto the sand, blood spurting from his eye socket.

For a moment, Zelda seemed stunned by her own actions. She stared down at the fallen man.

When she looked up, Brassington had his revolver pointed at her. "You little bitch," he said, and pulled the trigger.

He shot Zelda in the head, and she fell backwards onto the sand, her muscles coiling, and then a spasm rippled through her entire body.

Jasper sunk to his knees next to Zelda's body. "Holy… shit! What have you done?" Tears glossed his eyes, as he looked down at her. Zelda was pale, and her bare arms appeared bloodless. Despite the wound in her forehead, she still looked beautiful to him.

Jock watched on in shocked silence. "Norman…" he began, but he swiftly realised that Brassington had gotten caught up in his own, vengeful world, and was out of control. The big man still looked angry, rather than shocked or sad. "Norman, why?" Jock said softly. "She's your daughter."

"No daughter of mine," Norman said. He stared coldly into Jock's eyes. "Clean up this mess," he ordered.

"Norman—" Jock began tentatively.

"Clean it up," Brassington repeated, his voice barely above a whisper. "Clean it up, or leave."

"What do you—" Jock said, but he suddenly stopped. His gaze turned to Jasper, who was on his knees and bent over Zelda's body. "What about him?"

"Shoot him," said Brassington, and turned away, walking in the direction of the helicopter.

Jasper looked up at Jock. He was too exhausted to care about anything anymore. Brassington's command merely punctuated the inevitable. Without Zelda to speak on his behalf, he was as good as dead anyway.

Jock removed a pistol from his pocket, and stared at Jasper. He didn't relish the job of executioner.

"Turn around," Jock ordered. "Turn your back to me."

Jasper didn't bother to plead. Instead, he merely nodded and turned, facing Zelda. She appeared tranquil, finally without care or concern, he thought. He would be like that very soon.

He heard a faint sound as Jock clicked the safety off on his pistol. The sound instantly brought Jasper back to the present. He had no desire to die – he knew that. It simply wasn't fair. Most of his life was still ahead of him. He suddenly remembered Zelda's pistol, but realised almost in the same instant that it had been flung across the sand, too far out of reach. His brain kicked into overdrive, adrenalin coursing through his body.

"I'm a pilot," he suddenly announced.

"What?" Jock seemed surprised at the response.

"I'm a pilot. I can fly us out of here," Jasper said, sounding more confident.

Jock shook his head. "Even if you could... the helicopter is out of commission."

"I can fix it."

"I'd love to believe you—"

"I can fix it. I swear!" Jasper said desperately.

Jock remained quiet for a moment. Then Jasper heard him speak. "Norman." And then more loudly. "Norman!"

Jasper dared a look over his shoulder. He saw Brassington pause, and then stop. Jock took a few steps in his direction. "Norman, this man is a pilot. Reckons he can fix the chopper."

Jasper remained on his knees, and spotted something peculiar, right in front of him. A little piece of black plastic stuck out of the cast on Zelda's arm. Jasper leaned in closer and instantly recognised it as the edge of a credit card, with part of the number visible.

He touched the edge of the card with his fingers, then pulled it out. It was indeed a credit card, but unlike any he'd ever seen before. His thoughts were interrupted by the voices coming from behind him.

Brassington's voice was low and threatening. "If you disregard my instructions again, I will fucking kill you."

Jock was silent for a moment, before he responded. "What's happened to you, Norman?"

"Zelda didn't work out this little scheme by herself. You really want me to believe you had nothing to do with it?" Brassington sneered.

"Norman, you're losing your mind."

Brassington gave Jock a hateful stare and spat on the ground. "Get rid of your *pilot*," he said, and gestured towards Jasper. "Prove to me that you're worth it."

Jock hesitated. Then he nodded, turned, and walked purposefully towards Jasper, gripping the pistol tightly.

Jasper watched him approach. He clutched the credit card in his hand, without having any clear reason for doing so. *Because it belonged to Zelda?*

He lowered his head, pinched his eyes closed, and waited for the shot that would put him out of his misery – the shot that would erase all of his stupid mistakes in a single moment.

Two shots followed, in quick succession – but they were rifle shots, fired from across the beach. Jasper opened his eyes and stared at the wounds in Jock's chest and abdomen as the man fell backwards onto the sand.

Jasper watched the unfolding events in disbelief. *What was going on?* He couldn't understand why he was still alive.

At a rocky outcrop near the edge of the beach, he saw a man, ragged and dirty, carrying an AK-47 in his hands – the AK47 that had been stolen from him! It was the same man he'd seen coming ashore earlier, Jasper was sure of it.

The man walked with the AK-47 held combat style, ready to

deliver fast follow-up shots. He had a heavy limp. Jasper looked past Jock, lying in the sand bleeding and grunting. Further away, he noticed Brassington. The large man had turned around, and lifted his revolver... but his actions came far too late.

A short burst of gunfire took him down. Brassington, wounded but not yet dead, crawled over the sand, growling like a demented animal.

The shooter was closer now, and Jasper suddenly recognised him, despite the bearded face.

"Monty?" Jasper said. He was convinced he'd gotten trapped inside a bizarre dream. It *looked* like Monty, but that was impossible.

Monty looked at him without revealing any emotion, and walked on to where Jock lay. He shot Jock in the back of the head, finishing the job he'd started.

Brassington was still groaning and mumbling obscenities. Monty walked up to him, lifted the AK-47 and fired once at his head without the slightest hesitation. Brassington's groans stopped instantly.

Jasper slowly rose to his feet, holding his hands above his head. He expected to be next, but Monty showed barely any interest in him at all. He checked on the dead, and then came to stand in front of Jasper. His clothes were little more than rags, clinging to his body. He was barefoot and wore what was left of a khaki T-shirt and black shorts, or perhaps underpants – Jasper wasn't sure. He had scars on his face and other parts of his body, and his brow was swollen, as if he had suffered repeated beatings. But his eyes were still the same, flint-sharp and grey, just as Jasper remembered.

"Are you... going to shoot me?" Jasper's paralysing fear was back.

Monty looked at him curiously. "Not today, unless you annoy me," he said. He glanced at the deflated dinghy on the beach. "Is that all we've got?"

"I think so," said Jasper.

Monty looked at the motor yacht anchored offshore. "I guess we're swimming then," he said. He stopped nearer to take a closer look at Zelda. "That bitch nearly killed me."

"You… raped her!" Jasper said. The words slipped out before he could stop himself. He looked nervously at Monty.

Monty merely shrugged. "We had a thing before that," he said, and grinned at Jasper. "She liked the bad boys."

"You had… a thing?"

"Problem?" said Monty.

Jasper shook his head. He was struggling to reconcile the images flitting through his mind.

"You'll get over her," Monty said and turned away.

"We didn't… I mean I didn't have—"

"Whatever," Monty cut him short.

"How did you… survive?" Jasper asked after an awkward silence.

"Later," said Monty. His attention was fixed on the motor yacht, and on how they could get to it with the least amount of effort.

Monty dragged the corpses of the two men to the sea, and left them in the shallow waters for the crabs and other sea creatures to finish off.

Jasper followed his example. He grabbed Zelda's corpse by the wrists and dragged it towards the water, trying to overcome his revulsion, and his own guilt, for doing so. It was difficult to move the dead weight across the sand. Jasper sweated and groaned from exertion.

Pausing for a moment's rest, he sank to his knees next to Zelda's body. Her head had turned to one side, and he saw the nape of her neck, smooth and beautiful, just as he remembered it from their night together. Jasper noticed something unusual about the cast, now that her arms were above her body. With the underside of the cast exposed, Jasper noticed that there was a number scratched on it. He took a closer look: "156-948-226". *Clearly not a telephone number — but what could it be?*

Jasper felt the edge of the credit card against his fingertips inside his pocket.

"Need help?" Monty was suddenly right behind him, and the unexpected sound of his voice startled Jasper.

Jasper hurriedly stood up. "Ah... yeah," he said.

Monty looked at him strangely. "You should chill," he said without apparent humour.

Together, they dragged the body to the water's edge and released it to the sea. Jasper watched as Zelda's body drifted, face-up in the water.

She was floating free, her troubled life finally behind her.

59

"I was knocked out when I hit the water, but then the lights came back on and I swam like hell," Monty said, while they rested after dealing with the bodies. "Then a boat picked me up. Turned out they were a mob of smugglers. Tied me up, beat the shit out of me."

"Holy crap," said Jasper. "How did you get away?"

Monty shook his head. "I told them I worked with people who'd pay good money to get me back. They believed it, and kept me on their boat."

"How did you know we were here?"

Monty shrugged. "I didn't. This is one of their usual stops. They pick up water and stuff."

"What happened then?"

"They left me on the boat – with one man to guard me and the boat. That's when I got free, and escaped overboard. I heard some shooting. That's all I know."

"That's incredible," said Jasper. "So you were the one who stole my AK-47?"

Monty managed a small grin. "I watched you. You were like

a baby stumbling in the woods."

"Thanks," said Jasper. He grinned sheepishly.

Monty groaned as he got up, pressing down on his injured leg. "Let's go," he suggested.

Jasper too, rose to his feet, and followed Monty to the water's edge. They waded into the shallow water and began swimming towards the motor yacht.

The water was beautifully cool, and it made Jasper feel refreshed. He was more than happy to leave the island behind him, but realised the place would be forever etched in his memory.

They swam hard, diving under two breakers to reach the open water, but at least the motor yacht was within relatively easy reach.

Monty swam ahead, even though his injured leg prevented him from swimming very fast, and Jasper followed closely. Behind them, they could hear the breakers still crashing onto the beach.

Something very large broke the surface near to their position. The shark appeared out of nowhere, and in its attack, lifted Monty clear out of the water. The heavy weight of fish and prey crashed back down into the water, disappearing under the waves and leaving behind a frothy cloud of bubbles on the water's surface.

Monty's upper body reappeared above the surface a couple of seconds later, his hands clawing at the air as he desperately tried to swim away from the shark. The shark's second attack took him beneath the surface again, and Jasper saw blood bubbling upwards.

Jasper's mouth opened and closed in horror. He wanted to

scream, to shout, but his voice died in his throat. His first instinct was to swim for the beach as fast as he could – but then he realised that the motor yacht was so much closer.

Pure, frantic panic and a surge of adrenalin did their work. In a desperate bid for survival, he swam for the motor yacht with large, powerful strokes. He swam so fast it felt as if his arms would tear right out of their sockets.

Jasper didn't look back. He heard more thrashing in the water behind him, but refused to look, or to pause for even a second. The stern of the motor yacht loomed large in front of him. A few last, frantic strokes took him up close, and Jasper grabbed onto the small, half-submerged platform at the aft end of the yacht. Stepping onto it, he could reach the narrow stainless steel steps that led up to the deck. He grabbed one of the steps, hauled himself to his feet, and clambered hastily to the top.

He collapsed onto the deck, his chest heaving, his nerves shattered. When he stood up, he was hardly able to balance on his unsteady legs.

The fin of the shark was briefly visible above the water's surface, but then it disappeared quietly into the depths. A pool of blood drifted in the water. There was no sign of Monty.

Jasper rested his weight against the bulkhead, trying to keep his balance. He stood there for several minutes, waiting. But nothing happened.

A seagull screeched overhead, while the motor yacht rose and dipped gently with the movement of the water. The weather was perfect.

60

Port Fenton, on the island of Coroma, was a left-over from the colonial era. The larger buildings followed a British design, while many of the clusters of houses bore marks of a Dutch heritage. The local market, however, had a distinctly Pacific-island flavour. Here you could buy fresh and dried fish, fruit and vegetables – including the sought-after local yams – and a variety of island-themed fabrics and bric-a-brac.

Jasper wound his way through a small throng, on his way to the main business centre. He had moored the motor yacht at the far end of the harbour, so as not to attract undue attention, and then set out towards the town, with its white-washed houses set dramatically against the hills.

He wore a pair of chinos and a light cotton shirt that he'd found on the yacht, together with a pair of retro-looking teardrop sunglasses, a yachtsman's cap, and a pair of very comfortable deck shoes. It seemed strange to be back on land, and stranger still to hide his face behind a fast-growing beard. Jasper had wanted to shave it off at first, but changed his mind. By his way of thinking, having a beard was a little bit like travelling incognito – and that's the way he preferred it.

He walked past numerous market stalls, and ignored the voices of the stallholders, urging him to buy while prices were low, or inviting him to sample their wares. He dodged reckless scooter drivers, avoided a couple of bicycle rickshaws and eventually found his way to the business centre.

A building with the name 'Summerfield Merchant Bank' loomed large across the street. It was one of the most impressive buildings in the vicinity, and it even had a kiosk-entrance with several automatic teller machines at its southern flank. Jasper entered, and found that the place was air-conditioned, even though it was still early.

He fingered the black credit card in his pocket, and felt its sharp edge against his thumb. Stopping at one of the automatic teller machines, he glanced briefly outside, but saw nothing out of the ordinary. With a trembling hand, he inserted the card into the slot, and waited. He expected the card to be rejected, or worse, swallowed and a polite though stern message to appear on the screen instructing him to visit one of the human tellers inside.

Instead, the message on the screen merely read: "Insert pin number."

Jasper keyed in the number: "156-948-226". He entered it quickly, again expecting the machine to object. But it didn't. He was prompted to select an action. Did he want to withdraw, deposit cash, acquire a financial statement? He selected 'withdraw' and then entered a token figure of four hundred dollars. Jasper thought it was too risky to put in an amount that might be deemed too high.

The screen blinked, the machine produced a faint whirring noise, and then took about fifteen seconds running through an apparent processing cycle – before returning the card and dispensing the cash in crisp new notes in the local currency.

Jasper removed the notes, his hands shaking. Sweat drenched his armpits, and his breathing was uneven. He unceremoniously stuffed the money into his pocket and turned to leave.

It worked. Holy shit, it worked!

Jasper walked briskly towards the exit, when he heard a voice behind him. "Hey man."

For a fraction of a second, he thought about ignoring it and walking on – but then changed his mind, and slowly turned. *Was it a security guard? Were they on to him already?*

"Hey man," the stranger said again. "You left your card."

Jasper gave him a bewildered look, until he realised the man was actually attempting to help him. The auto teller machine emitted a low beeping noise.

"I... thank you," he replied. "Jeez... I can't believe—" He walked back to the machine and yanked the card out of the slot, then turned to the stranger and smiled gratefully. "Thanks mate."

The stranger nodded. He appeared amused by Jasper's odd behaviour.

Jasper slipped the card into his pocket and left the building without looking back.

61

The two young boys were in a race to get to the door first. The older one whipped the door open, and immediately called out at the top of his voice: "Dad! It's Jasper!"

Without missing a beat, the younger one questioned him. "Why have you got that?" He pointed at Jasper's face.

"It's a beard, dummy," said the older one.

Stavros Kosta appeared in the background, and he stared openly at Jasper. "Jasper, my God."

Jasper grinned and shrugged.

"Come in, come in," said Stavros, gesturing with one of his large, hairy arms.

Jasper stepped into the house, and heard the boys squabbling behind him. "Stavros, I'm sorry… about everything."

"Nonsense, nonsense," said Stavros, putting an arm around Jasper's shoulders. "We're going to sort this out." He ushered Jasper towards the lounge, and shouted loudly. "Hey, Maria! Jasper is here!"

Maria appeared at the entrance to the kitchen. "Jasper, oh my God – look at you!" Maria looked as if she was close to tears.

She hugged Jasper with a warmth and intimacy that made him feel as if he too, belonged to the family.

"Get him a beer," Stavros suggested.

"I'm alright, really," Jasper protested.

"You sit," Maria insisted. "I'll bring you a beer."

The lounge was in a state of chaos as usual, with cushions strewn over the carpet, and one of the curtains torn and smudged.

"Boys, I want you to clean up this place!" Stavros shouted, but the boys ignored him.

Jasper stepped over a broken game console and sidestepped a stain on the carpet, and then followed Stavros outside to sit on the porch.

"We thought you were dead! I wanted to find your family, to tell them," said Stavros. "But Brian said we should call the police."

Jasper lifted an eyebrow. "You called your lawyer first?"

Stavros shrugged. "You know, with the insurance and everything. You have to report it properly... so we can get the money."

"What did they say, the insurance people?" said Jasper.

Maria stepped outside, and handed Jasper a chilled bottle of beer. "What about a little something to eat?" she asked.

"Not for me, really," Jasper said. He knew Maria was capable of preparing an entire meal at the slightest hint of hesitation on his part. "I've eaten plenty, promise," he added.

She finally nodded, and disappeared back into the house.

"You sure you won't eat something?" Stavros asked.

Jasper shook his head. "What about the insurance?" he asked again.

"Well, you know," said Stavros with a little grin. "My brother in law, he organised a good deal for us. He says it's going to be alright. In some cases, they don't even investigate, he says."

"How are they going to investigate? The Goose is at the bottom of the ocean."

Stavros nodded. "Exactly the problem," he said. "I don't know how it all works. Brian said it was going to be alright. You must speak to him first – we may not need to go to the police..."

"What are the police going to do anyway?"

"It's all part of the policy, Jasper. The documents... it's complicated," said Stavros. "How's your beer going?"

Jasper shook his head. "Who's your insurance company?" he asked.

"They are, um..." Stavros searched his memory for the name. "Canaris... or something like that," he finally said.

"The company that was up for money laundering?"

"Jasper, these are... technical things, details. I don't know all the, how do you say, ins and the outs. I'm a businessman. Brian will sort it out for us, okay? Don't worry about it."

Jasper looked at him curiously for a moment, and then asked: "Stavros, are you going to buy a new plane?"

Stavros looked uncomfortable. "Jasper, you are like a... young brother to me, you know that?"

Jasper recognised that those words normally preceded bad news.

Stavros frowned. "It's just that the business, it's been... how do you say. It's been a bit up and down. This is not good business, my friend."

In the background the telephone rang, and moments later Maria appeared with the handset in her hand. "It's Bruce Andrews. He says you wanted him to call you," she announced.

"Bruce Andrews, the pilot?" Jasper said, surprised.

Stavros got up from his seat, and waved Jasper's question away with a motion of one hand. "It's business, Jasper, just business," he said by way of explanation, but Jasper knew instantly that Stavros had already been negotiating with the other pilot in Cornet Harbour.

"Are you sure you don't want a little something to eat?" Maria prodded, and Jasper again shook his head.

"Let me take this," said Stavros, excusing himself. "We'll talk. We'll talk some more."

Stavros entered the house, followed by Maria. Jasper was left by himself on the porch.

Jasper stood up, uncertain what to do next. Then he came to a quick decision. A future agreement between him and Stavros seemed out of the question. Clearly, it was time for him to leave.

As he stepped into the lounge, on his way to the front door, Jasper caught a news item on the large-screen TV that occupied an entire corner of the living room. He saw Zelda's photo on the screen, and snatched up the remote to turn up the sound.

"The millionaire businessman's daughter has also been reported missing, and an international police investigation is now underway," said the news announcer. "Zelda Brassington was last seen at a birthday party held for a friend. Interpol has now become involved in the ongoing search."

Jasper didn't hear the rest of the report. He was cold inside, and his mind involuntarily flashed back to the island, especially the time he had spent with Zelda. He walked to the front door as if in the middle of a dream.

Stavros's four-year-old son stood in the entrance hall, and looked at Jasper with a puzzled expression. "Where are you going?" he asked.

Jasper snapped out of his daydream, and looked down at the young boy.

"Away," he said, and left the house without saying goodbye.

62

Maybe one last withdrawal...

Jasper avoided the larger banks, and this time picked an automatic teller machine in a local shopping centre. It was a Tuesday, pension pay-day, and as expected he found a large number of pensioners in the centre, although the bank's automatic teller machine was free and, as far as Jasper could see, there were no security cameras in the vicinity.

He took the black credit card out of his pocket, and took another quick look around. A security guard was ambling in his direction. The man looked untidy and disinterested, with an ill-fitting uniform and buttons that strained to contain his large belly. Jasper paused. He glanced down at the shiny surface of the credit card, and for a brief moment saw his own face reflected back at him.

Worth the risk? Probably not.

The man didn't appear to be particularly vigilant, but Jasper decided to abort his final attempt to withdraw funds. The bank, and probably the police too, would be on to the withdrawals by now, he reasoned. He had enjoyed a good run, but it was time for him to get rid of the card.

He pocketed the credit card and left the shopping centre, walking back towards his car.

A young Chinese woman, smartly dressed in a grey business suit, her hair immaculately groomed, walked in his direction as he was about to cross the street. She was carrying a sheath of papers, and suddenly dropped them. Papers fluttered to the ground, and she looked embarrassed as she tried to pick them up – some of the papers already being dispersed by the wind.

Jasper paused and instinctively stooped to pick up some of the papers that had blown his way.

"Thank you so much," she said, touching his arm. In the commotion, she lost her balance slightly, and held on to Jasper for support. Jasper caught the scent of her sweet-smelling perfume, and her hair brushed against his face.

"I'm sorry," she said. "So sorry."

Jasper smiled at her. "No problem."

She scooped up another handful of papers, and then glanced at the pile of papers that Jasper had in his hands.

"I hope we've got them all," said Jasper.

She smiled back at him. "Thank you so much," she said again. "Can I ask you to… my car is right here," she said, pointing towards an expensive black Mercedes Benz parked in a loading zone a few metres away.

"Of course. Sure," said Jasper. He followed her to the car, and watched as she opened the back door.

"Just in there," she said. "Thank you so much."

The windows of the Mercedes were tinted dark, and it was impossible to see inside. As Jasper bent down to put the papers onto the back seat, he noticed a man sitting in the passenger seat on the opposite side.

The man wore an expensive business suit and silk tie, and he had an attaché case next to him on the seat. He smiled at Jasper. "Mister Owen?" he said.

Jasper was surprised that the man knew his name, and was immediately wary. He finally spoke. "Well, yes."

"My name is Chin Leung," the man said, offering Jasper a friendly smile. He had a faint British accent.

"I, um— Have we met?" Jasper asked.

The young woman opened the front door of the car, and leaned forward to pass a small, zip-locked plastic bag to Leung. In it was a small, black rectangular object. Jasper instantly recognised it – Zelda's credit card!

Jasper dug into his pocket, but could no longer feel the small plastic card. He'd been pickpocketed.

Leung looked at him in amusement. "We haven't met before, not face to face, at least," he said, still smiling. "Still, I think we have some mutual friends." He peered closely at the credit card in the sealed plastic bag. "Zelda Brassington, for example."

Jasper looked up at the woman next to him, and watched as she stripped a very thin, almost translucent glove off her left hand. Her hand was slim and appeared silky smooth. She wore no jewellery. The jacket of her business suit had opened just far enough for him to see that she was wearing a leather holster with a small-calibre pistol in it.

"Perhaps you'd like to have a quick talk... a chat," said Leung with a smile. "I would very much like to hear what happened on the island."

Jasper returned his attention to Leung, and realised that he again found himself in a position without any choices.

As if Leung was reading his mind, he said: "Blackmail does

not interest me, Mister Owen. I'm a businessman, and I think we may have something to talk about."

Jasper nodded tiredly, and then wordlessly seated himself in the back seat, next to Chin Leung.

The woman closed the passenger door on his side, and then took the driver's seat. Moments later, the Mercedes pulled away with a little squeal of tyres, and wound its way through the late-morning traffic.

Leung put Zelda's credit card into his inner jacket pocket, and when he noticed that Jasper was staring at it, he spoke. "I'm sure you'll have no further use for the credit, Mister Owen. I trust you made good use of it."

Jasper wanted to protest, but quickly thought the better of it.

Leung smiled at him. "I don't care about the money, Mister Owen. It does not belong to me."

Jasper nodded, and grinned bitterly.

"May I ask you what happened... in the last few weeks?" asked Leung.

Jasper hesitated for just a moment, and then replied. "You may, once you tell me how you're involved in all this."

"Fair enough," said Leung. "Tell me, have you met Norman Brassington?"

"Met? Yes," said Jasper, his mind flashing back to the moment on the beach when he came face to face with the man.

"Then you might know, he was not a very... pleasant person," said Leung.

"I gathered that."

"He was also not particularly pleasant in his business dealings, and as fate would have it, our paths crossed," said Chin Leung.

"Such people always have so many enemies; it is not difficult to find them. In Brassington's case, his enemies were very close. His daughter hated him, and his lieutenant, Jock Speller, plotted against him. Jock didn't have the stomach to go through with it, but Zelda did. Do you know what she did?"

"Faked her own kidnapping?"

Leung nodded. "Indeed. I put her in touch with a... someone who could help."

"Clive? You're talking about Clive Edgewood," said Jasper. "Fucking conman," he added.

"He was a bit... erratic, but I thought he'd get the job done. I was wrong."

"He was the one who pulled me in. He even sabotaged my job to get me to take that flight," said Jasper, flushed with anger.

"He can be very... persuasive," said Leung with apparent sympathy. "He told me he found a plane and pilot, and then said everything was under control. Until I heard that the plane went down, and Zelda was missing. Of course this was not part of the plan."

"Bloody right," said Jasper. "Clive put a psycho on board, who..." He stopped briefly mid-sentence, before continuing. "What difference does it make anyway?"

"Why don't you tell me what happened afterwards, on the island?" Leung said.

63

Belhaven, not too far from Cornet Harbour, was beautiful in the sunlight. By late morning, the sun created silvery ribbons on the water, teasing the eye with its live, rippling effect. A kingfisher swooped over the water, and the light breeze stirred up a cluster of reeds at the water's edge. It was perfect flying weather.

Jasper breathed deeply of the morning air. He had a cup of strong coffee in his hand, and looked out over the water, and then shifted his gaze to his pride and joy. The new floatplane was tied up to a small but well-constructed jetty, its bright orange-and-white paintwork glistening.

Jasper couldn't help smiling. It was all so perfect. And yet he couldn't help feeling slightly bored. But he had a feeling all that was about to change. His hand snaked around to the pistol that was tucked into the back of his pants. He touched the cool metal with his fingertips.

From the distance, he heard a car approaching – a large four-wheel-drive Lexus. The car stopped in a small cloud of dust, and a man opened the driver's door. He wore a shirt and tie, and sunglasses, and Jasper guessed the pants were part of an expensive suit.

"Mister Owen?" said the man. "You're the pilot, right?"

Jasper nodded. "Only one in Belhaven," he said.

"A friend mentioned your name," said the man. "I was looking for someone to take on a... special job, flying out to the islands."

Jasper's eyes narrowed, but then he smiled. "Why don't we discuss it inside?" he said, and pointed at the neat little shed that served as an office. It was located right next to his new hangar.

As they walked towards the shed, the man asked, "Is that your plane?"

Jasper glanced at the floatplane and smiled. "That's the one."

The aircraft had its name emblazoned near the nose, below the pilot's window. The name was written in flowing black letters: *'Zelda'*.

Don't miss *'Harrows Gate'* by Neil Colby

London 1989: Behind the walls of Harrows Gate lies a terrifying secret. A man who is falsely accused of murder escapes a brutal death by garrotting, only to find himself trapped in a depraved world of human experimentation. High-profile members of the London community are part of this dark conspiracy. A naive inventor and his assistant are the only ones standing in their way.

What's next?

If you have enjoyed this book and have a moment to spare, I would greatly appreciate a review. You can also sign up to be notified of new releases and giveaways, at:

neilcolby.com/sign-up

Emails are sent out infrequently, so they won't clutter your email inbox, and you can unsubscribe at any time.

About the Author

Neil Colby, a former film scriptwriter and newspaper sub-editor, lives in Sydney, Australia. He has travelled the world and notched up a number of unusual life experiences, including working in a hospital emergency room, and doing sound recordings in a war zone. He now writes books, embellishing some of his most memorable experiences and splicing them into his fictional stories.

www.ingramcontent.com/pod-product-compliance
Lightning Source LLC
Chambersburg PA
CBHW061602170626
46811CB00001B/292